SWEET TEMPTATION

She forgot what she'd planned to say. She only had to lean forward an inch or two to kiss him on the lips. She did, lightly. His mouth tasted earthily of sunshine, salt, and fish. She kissed him again, not so lightly this time. At first, he didn't kiss her back. When he did, he circled her ribs with his arms, pulled her so close she could feel the length of his thin body against her own, and kissed her long and slowly.

"Oh, Leenie," he groaned when he stepped back, "wild and lovely Leenie!" There was an ache in his voice that made Leenie reach for him again. "Leenie, Leenie, don't," he begged. "We can't do this . . ."

Avon Books are available at special quantity discounts for bulk purchases for sales promotions, premiums, fund raising or educational use. Special books, or book excerpts, can also be created to fit specific needs.

For details write or telephone the office of the Director of Special Markets, Avon Books, Dept. FP, 105 Madison Avenue, New York, New York 10016, 212-481-5653.

T2993

YESTERDAY'S DAUGHTER

Patricia Calvert

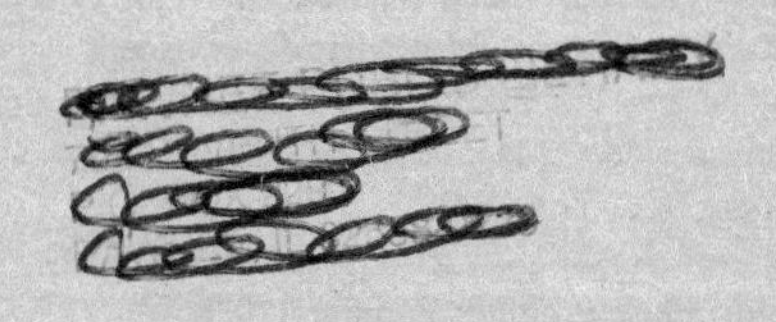

AN AVON FLARE BOOK

For
Brianne and Dana,
from
their mother,
with love

This novel is a work of fiction. Names, characters, places, and incidents either are the product of the author's imagination or are used fictitiously. Any resemblance to actual persons, living or dead, is entirely coincidental.

AVON BOOKS
A division of
The Hearst Corporation
105 Madison Avenue
New York, New York 10016

Copyright © 1986 by Patricia Calvert
Published by arrangement with Charles Scribner's Sons, a division of Macmillan Publishing Company
Library of Congress Catalog Card Number: 86-13753
ISBN: 0-380-70470-6
RL: 6.5

All rights reserved, which includes the right to reproduce this book or portions thereof in any form whatsoever except as provided by the U.S. Copyright Law. For information address Charles Scribner's Sons Books for Young Readers, Macmillan Publishing Company, 866 Third Avenue, New York, New York 10022.

First Avon Flare Printing: February 1988

AVON FLARE TRADEMARK REG. U.S. PAT. OFF. AND IN OTHER COUNTRIES, MARCA REGISTRADA, HECHO EN U.S.A.

Printed in the U.S.A.

K-R 10 9 8 7 6 5 4 3 2 1

1

Leenie O'Brien opened the screen door of the Big Cabin and peered out. Perfect. The beach was deserted except for the bottom half of a little girl's red swimsuit and a broken blue sand pail. It was only five A.M.; all the people in the Little Cabins were still asleep. She wouldn't have to put up with any tourists for at least two more hours.

Without waiting for an invitation to tag along, Lucy McGee insinuated her sturdy blonde body between the doorjamb and Leenie's right knee. "Any girl with the fine old name of O'Brien ought to have a pup with a good Irish name, too," Granda had declared on that long-ago afternoon when they brought the dog home from Edgewood Kennels.

But Luce isn't a puppy anymore, Leenie reflected wryly, and if things were the way they should be, my name wouldn't be O'Brien, either.

Leenie watched the dog take up her customary morning rounds. Lucy's light-colored tail, which made Leenie think of a broom made out of maiden cane grass, parted the mist as the dog moved across the empty beach. Lucy always knows where she's going and what she'll do when she gets there, Leenie mused. Too bad I can't say the same for myself.

Leenie narrowed her dark eyes. "I swear that child has got eyes the color of cold coffee," she'd heard Gramma remark once. As usual, there'd been a frown in her voice. Maybe she hadn't meant to be cruel, any more than she'd meant to be overheard, but Leenie remembered the unspoken accusation that had darkened her grandmother's words: you are an intruder in our lives, a person we never planned on, someone who's responsible for the color of her eyes.

Leenie inched the screen door open wider and hoped its hinges wouldn't squeak. Will it help, she wondered, if I try to concentrate my mind on what's over there across the water?

But the familiar, solid wall of straw-colored maiden cane grass that ordinarily was visible on the opposite side of Hadley Lake was shrouded in fog. That wall marked the perimeter of Sawmill Swamp, which drained into the lake, and simply to catch sight of it usually had the power to make her feel okay—for a little while at least—about a person named Leenie O'Brien.

Of course this morning it wasn't merely the fog, which kept a view of the swamp from her, that made everything else seem slightly out of focus. Mostly, Leenie realized, it was what Granda had read aloud from the letter he'd gotten yesterday that was to blame. After yesterday, life at the Dew Drop Inn (*You're Welcome Anytime, Just Like Kin* read the slogan at the bottom of the sign Granda'd put up at the junction of Highway 82 and County Road 12) might never be the same again.

Well, the first tip-off about that letter was the astonished way Granda held it in his sunburned hand after the mailman left. The second was the envelope itself: it was the color of vanilla ice cream (in Leenie's nightmares it had always been that color), and the writing on it had been done in chocolate-brown ink. To watch Granda stare down at it, though, bemused and smiling, had been confirmation of her worst suspicions. Her heart had shriveled to the size of a bog button.

It's finally happened, Leenie told herself, just like I always knew it would.

"Why, I do b'lieve this is from Mary Alice," Granda murmured finally. There was an echo of forgotten happiness in his voice Leenie didn't want to admit she'd heard. When he took up his brass letter opener—it was shaped like a swordfish and she'd helped him pick it out when they went down to Key West to go fishing the month after Gramma died—he made a neat incision down the spine of the envelope just as he might've made down the belly of a bluegill if he'd been cleaning one.

He laid the letter flat on his desk, and Leenie had to resist the temptation to stick her fingers in her ears when he started to read out loud.

"Dear Daddy," he began.

Daddy? Did Mary Alice actually still call him a little-kid name like that? It was crazy. Worse, it wasn't fair—she was too old for that now! The truth was, she'd long ago forfeited her claims on him, especially the one that said she had any right to call him a sentimental name like Daddy.

"Dear Daddy," Granda repeated, eager to savor the greeting again. The sunlight on his white hair made it gleam like the meringue on one of Hazel's lemon pies just before she popped it into the oven to brown. Leenie squinched her eyes shut; maybe if she couldn't see anything she wouldn't be able to hear anything, either.

"I realize this news might come as a shock to everyone down home," Granda read on, "but I have decided to come back for a visit at the end of the month."

Leenie opened her eyes. She peered over Granda's shoulder and saw the words for herself. Was Mary Alice giving them three weeks' notice in hopes somebody would volunteer to organize a "Welcome Home" committee in her honor? Did she expect marching bands, bouquets, red balloons?

Such a homecoming notion was totally off the wall. For starters, Jack O'Brien was called Granda now, because that's what he'd been for sixteen years. Another thing—if Mary Alice hadn't bothered to show up for Gramma's funeral two years ago, what in the world made her think anybody wanted to see her now?

"I've been thinking about it a lot, Daddy, and I've finally decided the time has come for all of us to put the past behind us," Granda continued, as delighted to be reading such words as Leenie was dismayed to be hearing them. "Maybe if we try real hard, we stubborn, headstrong O'Briens can learn how to be a regular family again."

Don't bet the rent on it, lady, Leenie wanted to advise her. This family is regular enough without you, thanks a bunch. You didn't want us sixteen years ago and now we don't want you, okay? Then she noticed that a vague, sweet smile still haunted the corners of Granda's mouth. Correction, Leenie amended; *I* don't need you.

But where did Mary Alice get off giving anybody advice about the past? I, for one, Leenie wanted to inform her, have not been hanging around here with my shoelaces tied together waiting for a green light about *that*. "We should put the past behind us," she mocked under her breath. "For your information, madam, I want to remember mine, just so I never end up doing what you did."

Leenie let the screen door shut softly behind her. It was weird, she reflected, how when things started to go haywire—such as having a letter arrive like that one did yesterday—then a person could usually expect lots of sour things to happen all day long. For sure that'd been true yesterday. Take, just for instance, the program that came on TV right after supper.

Hazel had finished up the dishes and had taken the bus back to her own place in Wayburn, five miles away, so Leenie decided to watch a show about the county animal shelter. Granda watched, too. Very innocent, right? Well, he had a problem, admitted the animal warden. It appeared that a lot of people had taken to dumping off cats and dogs in the ditches beside Highway 82 that ran northeast past Wayburn and went all the way up to Savannah.

The warden surmised that certain folks' pets had seemed like cute, cuddly things to bring home at Christmastime but had gotten to be pains in the neck to take care of by Eastertime, so they'd just plain been abandoned. Here it was, he lamented, practically midsummer, but he still had at least a half dozen orphaned pets that needed new homes, including a large white rabbit that wore a red leather collar that said its name was Harold. As he spoke, an assistant was shown holding poor Harold, who gazed at the camera with soulful pink eyes.

Granda admitted with a yawn that yes, it truly was a pity the careless way some folks behaved, but wasn't Lucy McGee a lucky old pooch to have two people to love her and to get table scraps for supper every night. Which was true, Leenie agreed silently, but so was something else that Granda didn't especially want to mention.

It isn't only kittens and puppies and rabbits named Harold that get dumped when they're too much trouble to take care of, Leenie wanted to remind him during the commercial. Sometimes people get rid of their own kids. All of which Mary Alice O'Brien now wanted to refer to lightly as the past.

Leenie rested her knobby backbone against the screen door. The mist wetted her cheeks and made her dark hair cling damply to her forehead. It hadn't taken anything terrible like an earthquake or a hurricane to turn the summer upside down, she realized. All it'd taken was a one-page letter from Boston. That vanilla-colored envelope she'd dreamed about so often had finally arrived; its contents had been read out loud; there was no way to pretend the mailman hadn't stopped yesterday.

Would it help to say a small prayer? Leenie wondered. She wasn't exactly sure she believed in the power of that stuff anymore. "Give me a break," she ventured softly, just in case it still worked.

"Maybe Mary Alice had a baby sixteen years ago," she explained, "but that never really made her a mother. I mean, a mother is a person who sticks around, right?" Leenie waited for a signal out of the mist that Somebody up there was paying attention. No signal came, but she went on anyway.

"Now Mary Alice says she wants to put the past behind her," Leenie whispered. "Trouble is, I'm the kid who belongs to all those yesterdays she says shouldn't matter anymore. So whoever You are up there, please don't let her come home, okay? Thank You. Amen."

2

Leenie followed Lucy McGee's tracks across the deserted beach toward the bright yellow lifeguard's tower that stood at the edge of the lake.

It'd been hot last night, so she'd dug an old sleeveless nightgown out of a corner in the closet where she'd tossed it a long time ago. She put it on in the dark, glad for its gossamer feel against her bare skin. The gown was covered with fat pink unicorns and now, in the pale light of morning, Leenie could also see that it was several inches shorter than she remembered it to be. No problem. All the tourists were still asleep. She'd be into a pair of clean cut-offs and a decent T-top before any of them were up to face the day.

A large wood sign hung by two metal chains from the painted yellow legs of the tower and warned NO LIFEGUARD ON DUTY. Leenie turned it around so that it declared LIFEGUARD ON DUTY and climbed the ladder into the tower. She lowered herself into the striped canvas chair Granda occupied every morning and that she took charge of herself each afternoon. She propped her elbows on her knees and peered into the mist. Now, an edge of gold had become faintly visible on the far side of Hadley Lake.

If I were a stranger in this place, Leenie mused (or a person just marking time before I moved on to somewhere else like Gramma always believed I was), then I'd figure that yellow wall across the water might be the edge of an island. Or maybe I'd think it was a finger of land—Granda would call it a spit—that reached into Hadley from the opposite shore.

Except I know better, Leenie thought. Sure ought to, anyhow, after sixteen years. The truth was, there wasn't an opposite shore to the lake. That wall of maiden cane marked the melting together of lake and swamp, and for Leenie it'd always been the swamp, not the lake, that mattered most.

"First time I rowed out there with you, you weren't any bigger'n a gnat's eyebrow," Granda liked to remind her. To him, she'd never been a person who didn't belong. "Bet you know the swamp now almost as well as I do," he liked to tease. "Why, if somebody wanted a guide for Sawmill, you'd be the best!" It was true: she'd explored it from one end to the other, knew by heart the location of every egret's nest, the interior of each gloomy cypress bay, the boggy feel of every tiny island.

For the past few years she hadn't had to wait for Granda to take her out there, either. She could go alone in the cypresswood punt he'd designed and built for her twelfth birthday and had christened the *Swamp Rat.* He liked to hang names on things—dogs, boats, kids. Gramma said he was the one who'd come up with the nickname Leenie, too. Even now, four years after that birthday, Leenie could feel the weight of her grandfather's wide hand on her shoulder and hear the words he'd whispered.

"It's yours, Leenie McSweeney McFeeney McBeeney," he'd confided softly so Gramma couldn't eavesdrop, "so you can go exploring any old time you feel like it and get yourself all the peace and quiet you need."

Leenie knew what he wanted to say, might've tried to say if Gramma hadn't been right there, frowning. "I love you, Leenie O'Brien," he would've said, "and I don't care two hoots or a holler how you got into this world." With Gramma, of course, things weren't so simple. Even as she lay dying, she'd never asked about Mary Alice, never wondered if maybe her only daughter would come home.

Leenie scratched at a mosquito bite and tried to refocus her attention on the yellow wall across the water. It was hard to do, though. The words from yesterday's letter refused to stay still; they kept rolling around inside her head like loose marbles on a tin plate. One thing you had to admit, however: the P.S. Mary Alice had tacked onto her letter really took a lot of nerve.

"Please, Daddy," she'd written in her chocolate-colored ink, "tell Arlene that I think of her oftener than she'll ever know."

Arlene? She had to be kidding. Here's a P.S. for you, Leenie thought bitterly. Everyone around here calls me Leenie—everyone who matters, that is. But what did Mary Alice know about anything? Not very much, that's how much.

Like for six Christmases in a row she'd sent a doll. A doll—for a person who liked to pole a punt named the *Swamp Rat* and knew secret places beyond the wall of maiden cane that even Granda didn't know about? Bad judgment, lady; very bad.

Those dumb dolls were never played with, though, not even once. They were still on the shelf in the closet, tall dolls and short dolls, soft squishy dolls and one hard plastic doll with silly little boobs molded onto her narrow chest. Only a dimwit who didn't know one single thing about *me* would've sent any of 'em, Leenie had concluded a long time ago.

Some of the packages Mary Alice had sent for birthdays had never been opened at all. Leenie had written messages on their brown wrappers in bold letters with a red felt-tip pen she got out of the desk in Granda's office.

"Unknown at This Address!" she'd scribbled, or "Return to Sender!!!" with rows of exclamation marks that looked like bullets. For a long time those packages lay on the closet shelf along with the dolls. Too bad Mary Alice didn't know all that. If she did, she wouldn't be so crazy to get back home again.

Leenie scraped at a second mosquito bite and propped her right ankle across her left knee. It was probably a good thing she'd only been three months old when Mary Alice decided to leave, though. What did a three-month-old kid care, anyway? Babies that age just ate and slept and messed their diapers. It would've been a lot more painful if she'd been, say, five or six years old when Mary Alice took a powder. A kid that age might've been lonesome and cried for days and taken up all kinds of nervous habits, just like Hazel's niece Bitsie did after her dad died.

With me, it's a lot different than what happened to poor Bitsie, Leenie reflected. After all, how could I miss someone I never knew in the first place?

From her perch in the tower, Leenie watched Lucy McGee walk into the lake. Being a Chesapeake retriever, Lucy naturally loved the water almost as much as she loved a good rib bone for supper. Even though the man at the kennel had wanted to sell her, he'd taken pains to point out all her bad qualities. He didn't want any dissatisfied customers, he explained. Never mind, Granda had assured him; we want a buddy, not a dog who has to win blue ribbons to make us happy.

"Good, on account of that's one thing this dog will never be able to do for you," the man was determined to say. "Look there. She's got herself a bunch of dark freckles on her nose and more of 'em on her feet. Ideal Chesapeake, you know, has got to be a solid color, preferably a shade they call deadgrass in the dog books," he rattled on, "and in my opinion this dog is a-way too light-colored." Granda was firm; all she has to do is love the water as much as Leenie and me, he'd said, paid the man fifty dollars, and walked to the car with the pup tucked under his arm.

"Hey, Luce, you old freckled failure," Leenie called down softly from her perch. Lucy McGee looked up and gave Leenie an unapologetic snort. Her eyes were light-colored, too, just about the same shade as the sun tea that Hazel liked to brew every summer. Lucy lay down in the shallow water at the foot of the lifeguard's tower, rolled over, and with all four feet in the air proceeded to scrub her backbone in the sand.

Leenie took time to torment a scab on her right knuckle. Well, considering yesterday's bad news, there was still one thing to be grateful about: none of the folks who came to stay at O'Brien's Dew Drop Inn, located five miles from Wayburn on Highway 82, ever cared a whit about Sawmill Swamp, much less Sugar Island way out there in the middle of it.

What most tourists wanted was just a cheap place to stay for a few days or a week, a bit of clean beach for sunbathing, some safe water for their kids to paddle around in without getting drowned. People who had lots of money whizzed right past the Dew Drop and headed for Turtle Beach over on the Carolina coast, or else they went straight down Highway 23 to Miami, which had lots of glitz and glitter.

It was ordinary people—plumbers and store clerks and postmen from little towns in Illinois or Colorado or Idaho—who stopped at the Dew Drop who were the main reason Leenie got tired of the $eason, however.

That's what Granda called it, the $eason, with the S made into a dollar sign. There were four parts to the year, he liked to say, Fall, Winter, Spring, and the $eason, which began in May and lasted almost till Thanksgiving, depending on the weather. Now that lots of people were buying motor homes with names like Southwind or Safari, though, there were times when some of the cabins at the Dew Drop stayed empty for a week or two at a time, so it didn't make a lot of sense to get irritable with tourists.

"Let me remind you those folks are our bread-and-butter, Leenie McQueenie," Granda had cautioned her more than once, "and without 'em, you and me couldn't afford to live here the other five months of the year."

The $eason was the reason she had to get up so early all summer, though. It was the only time a person could find a little private time. Now, at five A.M., people on vacation from Springfield or Boulder or Pocatello were snoring their brains out in their rented cabins, but just wait till nine o'clock—the sandy beach on either side of the yellow lifeguard's tower would be littered with strangers' bodies in various stages of burn, peel, and tan. Little kids would be running all over the place in swimsuits no bigger than Band-Aids. But sometimes those kids were a stitch to watch: one of 'em would suddenly peel off his or her suit and go shrieking el nudo among the startled sunbathers until captured in a towel by a flustered parent.

The mist began to rise off the water like smoke; soon the sun would be rising. Leenie squinted, hoping thereby to bring the swamp closer. She wasn't exactly surprised when the trick didn't work very well. Best thing to do, she realized, would be to jump right into the *Swamp Rat* and go out there for real.

"Which definitely is what I'll do," Leenie informed Lucy McGee, "if that person who calls herself my mother sticks to her crazy plan to come back here where she doesn't belong." After all, hadn't Mary Alice done enough damage, giving birth to an illegitimate kid, then dumping it on her own parents?

Illegitimate; what a weird word. Gramma'd gotten all bent out of shape and her mouth got that pinched, don't-you-dare-say-another-word-about-it look the day Leenie asked what it meant. After that, she naturally was too scared to ask Granda, either. The only other person she knew who might be able to tell her what it meant was Hazel. It seemed like Hazel always knew something about practically everything.

"Oh, sweet cakes, who ever laid a word like that on you?" Hazel wanted to know right away. She was turning a mattress in cabin nine when Leenie finally tracked her down. She was wearing her favorite baby-blue sweat shirt imprinted with a large yellow croppie and a message underneath that declared *I Wish I Was Fishing.*

"Sooz said her mom told her that's what I am. Illegitimate, that's what she said. What's it mean, Hazel?" That had been the second week of third grade. Walking home from the bus, Leenie had decided the word made it sound like she was illegal, a person the government might decide to deport. Only where would they send her? She didn't want to go to Mexico, but maybe Canada wouldn't be too bad. Granda said once that the bass fishing up around Thunder Bay, Ontario, was the best in the world. Maybe he could even come up and visit her sometime.

"What it means, honeybun, is a person whose folks didn't happen to be married when that person was born," Hazel explained.

"Like my mother wasn't married when she had me, right?"

"You got it, sweet pea. Which is not the end of the world, may I add, and it sure doesn't make you less of a person than Sooz herself. You hear me?" Hazel had taken time to smooth back Leenie's dark bangs before she tucked a pair of pillows into fresh, starched pillowcases.

Leenie pulled her bangs back even with her eyebrows where they belonged. "Were your mom and dad married when you were born, Hazel?"

"Well, yes," Hazel admitted with a groan, "for the record, they were. But like I told you, that doesn't mean that you aren't just as—"

Leenie escaped before Hazel could ladle up further assurance. There were times, even if you were only in third grade, when a person had to go off and be alone. Having just found out that you really were illegal, that your best friend wasn't just being spiteful again, was one of those times.

Leenie remembered that afternoon very well: it was September and Granda had already turned some of his boats over on cement blocks so they could dry out and be given a fresh coat of paint before winter set in. She'd crawled under one and lain there in the silent, spidery dark until suppertime. It had been a good place to feel sorry about the way you'd gotten into the world.

But I'm too old now to crawl under an upside-down boat, Leenie realized. This time I'll have to find someplace else to go.

"Hey, Luce," Leenie whispered, "how do you feel about taking a little vacation?" Lucy, who was busy shaking water out of her heavy coat, didn't reply.

"It isn't like we'll be the first ones who ever went into the swamp to hide out," Leenie told her. Lucy lifted one pale ear. Sawmill Swamp had opened its arms to others who were on the run—Civil War deserters, runaway slaves on their way to freedom up north, bank robbers who'd sawed their way out of jail—so why wouldn't it welcome a person the rest of the world called illegitimate? Especially if that person wanted to punish the one who'd made her illegal in the first place?

"She must think I'm a sucker," Leenie confided to Lucy. The dog raised both ears. "Mary Alice has this idea, see, that she can come back here and pretend she never dumped me like I was a pet she got tired of. She treated me like garbage, Luce, only I was too little to do anything about it. But now I can, and you know what I'm going to do?"

Leenie paused and savored her revenge and was pleased at how sweet it tasted. "I'm going to bail out on Mary Alice just like she bailed out on me, Luce. You and me'll just pack up and—"

A small, soft splash near the left side of the tower caused Leenie to turn and frown. A few feet down the beach someone was easing a boat into the water. Granda didn't allow any motorboats on the lake; instead, he supplied each cabin with a flat-bottomed rowboat, painted pale green to match the cabins, the kind of craft that wouldn't tip over easily and leave him open to a lawsuit in case some clumsy tourist got drowned.

Leenie planted her feet flat on the slatted floor of the lifeguard's tower and scrunched herself way down in the canvas chair. She tugged the fat pink unicorns as far over her knees as they would willingly go. Wouldn't you know it? Some freaky tourist was up already—but it wasn't even six A.M. yet!

Gloomily, Leenie watched the boat move farther out into the lake. Her frown turned to a scowl. Oh. It was him. The character who'd rented cabin twelve. He'd driven up about four days ago in a dusty brown van, said he wanted to rent a cabin for a whole month, which made Granda's eyes positively shine. He was alone, which seemed peculiar, and he was from New York State, which made him even odder.

Two other details set him apart from the ordinary, generic-type tourist, Leenie remembered. First, he was about the same age as Sooz's brother Buck who was going to Wayburn Vo-Tech to learn how to be an electrician. Second, although he was young, he had old eyes about the color of gravel, and a sidelong way of looking at a person, as if he knew things about you he wasn't entitled to know. She'd made up her mind, then and there, to steer clear of him.

Now that he was dressed only in a pair of cut-offs and tennies, Leenie observed that the tourist was also so skinny a person could've played "This Old Man" on his ribs. He didn't have a good tan yet, but wore epaulets of freckles on his shoulders, and the damp morning air had caused his cinnamon-colored hair to crimp into tight, corkscrew curls all over his head.

The tourist chopped clumsily at the water with his paddles. Does he think it froze overnight and now he's got to chop holes in it? Leenie wondered. He also must figure feathers were only for ducks, because he obviously didn't know how to feather a paddle, either. Pretty soon, though, he'd lose himself in the mist that was being turned the color of ripe peaches by the rising sun. Then she'd just sneak down out of the tower and—

But Skinny Ribs stopped paddling. He rested his oars in their locks and just sat there, staring hard toward the swamp, his elbows propped on his bent knees.

Leenie waited. A moment later, the tourist reached into the bottom of his boat and picked up something. He fiddled with it, then held it up to his eyes. He scanned the horizon in a wide arc and stopped when his face was turned toward hers.

Slowly, it dawned on Leenie what was happening: he had a pair of binoculars and he was spying on her.

"Nerd!" she wanted to shout. "Mind your own beeswax!" It was chilling to imagine what she must look like viewed through those twin lenses, perched as she was in the yellow tower, trying to cover her long, brown storklegs with a bunch of pink unicorns while her hair hung like dark, sleep-tangled ropes against her shoulders.

A terrible numbness started at Leenie's toes and crept toward her heart. There was no longer any doubt about it: this $eason was even worse than the one when Gramma died. Number one, Mary Alice O'Brien, who didn't ever deserve to be called Mother, was coming home to Wayburn. Number two, there was a nerd in cabin twelve and he planned to stay at the Dew Drop Inn for a whole month.

Leenie stared over the head of the tourist, who finally began to paddle toward the middle of the lake. Suddenly, the lure of Sugar Island, deep in the heart of the swamp, became even sweeter than its name.

3

It was only six-thirty when Leenie padded barefoot into the kitchen, but Hazel had already arrived and had some sausage in a pan. Soon the kitchen smelled like it had on mornings when Gramma was still alive.

Nevertheless, Leenie felt annoyed. She'd planned to sit by herself at the kitchen table and ponder her bleak future over a cup of warmed-over coffee. She couldn't drink coffee when Granda was around. He thought it was bad for her health and if he remembered (fortunately, he forgot most of the time), he emptied the pot into the sink before he went to bed.

"How come you got here so early?" Leenie complained. Hazel must've taken the first bus out of Wayburn to have arrived at the Dew Drop just as the sun was coming up.

"My, that's sure a sweet note I hear in your voice this morning. I suspect you're in another one of your swamp-rat moods," Hazel observed, and turned the sausages with a fork. "But, since you're so nosy, may I inform you I am on my way over to Decatur with my sister Jemma. I am going to buy a car, but couldn't find exactly what I wanted in Wayburn. I'm here early so Jemma and me can be on our merry way by noontime. Is that okay with you, Your Mightyness?"

As far back as Leenie could remember, Hazel had worked for Granda. Before Gramma died, Hazel did cabins just like Ruth and Eloise did now, which meant she scrubbed and vacuumed and changed bedsheets and put fresh toilet paper on the rolls and new soap in the soap dishes in each of the Little Cabins.

When Gramma got sick, though, Hazel started to cook meals for the family and keep Granda's office clean and sometimes wait on tourists. After Gramma was gone, Hazel didn't do much housecleaning except in the Big Cabin, with maybe a little bookkeeping on the side. Granda had even gotten her a yellow plastic name tag that read, "Hazel Grobey, Ass't. Mgr."

"I hope you don't have any special plans for yourself this morning," Hazel went on, ignoring the fact Leenie hadn't blessed the car-buying plans, "because Eloise called me last night and she's coming down with summer flu. Since Ruth is on vacation this week, you might have to give me a hand with a couple of the cabins, okay?"

Leenie folded her bones into a chair and groaned. Cleaning cabins was not anything she wanted to become habit-forming. Hazel paid no heed to the groan and laid sausages to drain on a folded paper towel, where they looked like tiny brown logs. Hazel had strong preferences and greasy sausage was not one of them. Next, she set two blue plates on the table and laid out paper napkins printed with daisies.

"How come only two plates?" Leenie grumbled. "I thought you said you weren't leaving until noon."

"It's not me who isn't eating breakfast, sugar. Your granddaddy left twenty minutes ago with that air conditioner from cabin eight. He's got to drive all the way to Columbus so's he can get it repaired under the warranty, but he hopes to be back by the time I leave with Jemma.''

Hazel's tennies squeaked on the floor as she turned back to the stove to scramble some eggs. The tennies were new but already had holes in their sides, Leenie noticed. ''You already got holes in the sides of those new tennies,'' Leenie pointed out.

''I put them there myself to give my bunions some growing room, so don't think you're telling me news I don't already know,'' Hazel informed her.

If there wasn't so much of her, her bunions wouldn't give her such fits, Leenie thought. There was no sense bringing that fact to Hazel's attention, though, because her opinion about dieting was even firmer than her opinion about greasy sausage.

''I am a generous woman,'' Hazel was fond of saying, ''and that includes my size, which is nobody's business but mine. Besides, a woman without meat on her bones is like a pillow without feathers.'' The latter was a bit of wisdom she'd passed on one afternoon when Leenie had been foolish enough to speculate how much certain people weighed.

Not that Hazel was fat. Hazel was as solid as an oak tree, and since she was nearly as tall as Granda, she seemed more majestic than pitiful. Added to that was the fact that since she worked in her garden at her own place in Wayburn, she always had a nice suntan. She was fifty-six years old, her eyes were the color of warm butterscotch, and she wore her carmel-gray hair in a ponytail that hung past her shoulder blades. When she was happy or going somewhere, she tied a ribbon around her ponytail instead of a plain old rubber band.

Today, Leenie noticed, a blue satin bow rested on Hazel's wide, sunbrowned neck. She's glad because she's going over to Decatur to buy a car, Leenie thought. Lucky her. All I have to do is sit around here and think about Mary Alice and el weirdo in cabin twelve.

It would really be nice if Hazel never had to go home anymore. She could forget about buying a car. She could sell her house in town and plant her garden at the Dew Drop Inn and grow tomatoes that would glow like traffic lights. The three of them, plus Lucy McGee, could live happily ever after.

"I've been thinking, Hazel."

"Congratulations. I predict a great future for you."

"I'm serious, Hazel. Why don't you move out here? Then you wouldn't need a car, which I doubt you can afford to buy anyway."

"The reason I can't afford one, sweet thing, is because I need a job that pays me better than what your Granda can afford to pay me. Besides, it would not be seemly for me to move out here."

"Seemly, schmeemly. You and Granda could get married. People as old as you guys get married all the time."

"Thanks for not also suggesting I buy a cemetery plot along with my marriage license. The truth is, your granddaddy and I do not want to get married." Hazel sat down at the table and beckoned Leenie to do likewise. "What put such a notion in your head, anyway?" she murmured. "This is the second time this week you've mentioned the subject of marriage."

"Most people want to get married," Leenie insisted. Well, Mary Alice hadn't, but did she count? No.

Hazel poured a golden ribbon of sorghum over a steaming corn muffin. "Your Granda and I are definitely out of the romance business, Leenie. He got wore out nursing your Gramma through her dying time and I got tired of bailing my Jeffrey out of jail and hanging him out to dry so often.''

''Hanging him out to dry?'' Leenie made a lumpy yellow mountain out of her scrambled eggs and tried to get a mental picture of what it must've been like to hang Jeffrey Grobey out to dry. Jeffrey had been tall and thin; maybe Hazel just grabbed hold of his feet, swung him up and over the—

''That's what it's called when an alcoholic is trying to quit drinking,'' Hazel explained. ''Drying out, that's what it's called; it doesn't mean clotheslines and clothespins. Now please eat your eggs.''

''Did he ever get dry?''

''Not in this life, sweet pea. You know perfectly well Jeff Grobey got himself run over five years ago at that train crossing near Decatur, which had the effect of permanently taking care of his troubles. Eat your sausage, Leenie; otherwise, you are in serious danger of turning into a pencil.''

''But Granda never drinks anything worse than a Pepsi once in a while, and you've never been sick like Gramma was, so the two of you might just as well—''

''Sweetie, give up this crazy matchmaking business,'' Hazel advised. ''I am not—hear me good—ever going to marry Jack O'Brien.'' She refilled her coffee cup and moved her chair back from the table. Leenie's breakfast cooled on her plate while she got up and fidgeted aimlessly about the kitchen.

''I've been thinking, Hazel.''

''So you mentioned. Sounds to me like you plan to make it a regular hobby.''

Leenie cracked her knuckles. Sooz said you got big, knobby knuckles if you did that, but what did big knuckles matter to a swamp rat? ''I think I will take a little trip out to Sugar Island,'' she murmured. She watched Hazel to see what effect the news might have. As expected, Hazel's butterscotch gaze grew narrow and thoughtful.

"I don't suppose that letter your granddaddy got yesterday has anything to do with your sudden travel plans."

"Letter?" Leenie lifted one shoulder and managed to look astonished. "Oh. You mean that one from . . ." She let her words trail away.

"Indeed I do, missy. I mean the letter from Mary Alice."

Leenie circled the table. She'd seen a tiger once, in a zoo in Florida. It had circled the cage, its amber eyes brooding, had acted like it never wanted to rest. She, on the other hand, was already tired of pacing around the kitchen. Hazel's blue denim apron, spread over her ample knees, made her lap seem the size of a card table. Leenie rested her haunches on Hazel's right knee, then gave up and crawled onto Hazel's lap. She buried her nose against Hazel's warm brown neck.

"Leenie, you are getting too big to be climbing on me like this," Hazel objected mildly. Leenie folded herself up until she was as small as she could get, which wasn't easy since she was already nearly as tall as Hazel.

"I'm not too big yet," she mumbled against Hazel's collarbone. "See, I still fit. Almost."

Hazel draped a pair of large brown arms around Leenie and patted her bony hip the same way Leenie sometimes patted Lucy McGee's rear end.

"Did you know her, Hazel?"

"Who her?"

"Mary Alice O'Brien."

"Sure I knew her. She was a pretty girl. Nice, too."

"*Nice?* Then how come she—"

"Got preggers before she got married?" Hazel spoke sympathetically of matters like drying out and getting pregnant. Gramma sure could've taken a few lessons from Hazel, Leenie reflected. "Well, sweet pea, I don't know the answer to that," Hazel went on. "Maybe Mary Alice doesn't either."

"Which brings me to another point."

"I was afraid it might."

"Like, Hazel, who was my father?"

"I don't know the answer to that either, Leenie, truly I don't. See, Mary Alice was only seventeen years old when all that came down, and I was just a maid here at the Dew Drop. It was natural that she didn't regard me as her best buddy or feel free to confide something to me that she didn't even tell her own folks."

"Gramma and Granda never knew either?"

"Not as far as I know."

"Maybe Mary Alice didn't know who he was," Leenie muttered. "Maybe she made out with so many guys that—"

"Leenie, Leenie. Enough already. Mary Alice O'Brien, in my opinion, was a nice girl who made a mistake. Didn't you ever?"

Leenie considered the possibility. "Nope. Well, wait. Maybe once. Last year in geography. I couldn't remember the capital of Rumania. I put down Silistra. It's Bucharest."

"My, my. Aren't you a regular paragon of virtue? Pass me that halo so I can polish it a little brighter for you." Hazel adjusted her knees and consulted her watch.

"Whoops—time for me to get a wiggle on," she announced. With a pair of large brown hands she lifted Leenie up and set her on her own two feet. "I'll do up these breakfast dishes and take care of cabin nine if you'll take care of the other one. Okay?"

A long, mournful look must've crossed her face, Leenie decided later, because Hazel took her by the hand and whispered, "Know what, sugar? You got the same problem my poor old Jeffie had. You got the notion somewhere that life ought to be quality controlled. You think it ought to be pasteurized, homogenized, have vitamin D added and meet all daily minimum requirements. Wake up, sweet cakes—sometimes life is liable to get itself hauled down to the police station on a disorderly conduct charge. Like I told Jeffrey R. Grobey, 'The rainbow comes and goes, baby.' "

Leenie wanted to plug her ears. She didn't need a lecture, not even one from Hazel. Hazel squeaked across the floor in her holey tennies and plucked two keys off the rack on the wall near the office door. She dropped one of them in her apron pocket.

Well, maybe cleaning a cabin would keep her from thinking about rainbows or people who were determined to come home to Wayburn where they didn't belong, Leenie decided. Hazel laid a key in her palm and Leenie stared down at it, dismayed.

"Better close that mouth, sweet thing," Hazel advised, "otherwise you are going to swallow yourself a fly." Leenie felt cool, as if she'd just stepped lightly out of her own skin. She closed her mouth and folded her fingers around the key to cabin twelve.

4

Of all the Little Cabins at the resort, cabin twelve was the smallest and it had always been Leenie's favorite.

In the off-$eason, when she'd been nine and ten and there wasn't a tourist within two hundred miles of the Dew Drop, she'd go over there and pretend it was a playhouse. Later, when she was thirteen and fourteen, she sometimes warmed a can of soup for herself on chilly afternoons after school, then settled down to read one of Hazel's novels. Hazel always read the same kind of book. On the cover there'd be a dark mansion with a scared-looking girl wearing a pale dress that had one shoulder torn loose running out of the front door. Hazel called such books bodice-rippers and bought a new one every Friday at Walser's drugstore in Wayburn.

Granda had built cabin twelve, just like he'd built all the others at the Dew Drop. It had three tiny pine-paneled rooms, the sweetest of them being the living room, which had a fireplace he'd crafted out of native stone. He'd embedded pieces of colored glass in the grout that held the stones together, and in the evening when she stopped at cabin twelve for a cup of tea, the glass chips gleamed cozily in the lamplight.

It was honeymooners most of all, though, who liked cabin twelve, partly because it was like a dream house, partly no doubt because it was separated from the other cabins by a pretty dogwood hedge. No honeymooners bent on privacy could rent it now, Leenie reflected. Old Skinny Ribs had grabbed it for a whole month.

Leenie wheeled a utility cart out of the maintenance shed next to the garage. She loaded it with fresh sheets and pillowcases. She added towels from the cupboard behind the door of the shed. She stacked up soap, a couple rolls of toilet paper, and filled a spray bottle with glass cleaner from a gallon jug of Glass-B-Brite.

She'd groaned out loud about having to take Eloise's place (Leenie knew perfectly well that Eloise didn't have the flu; it's what she said every time she decided to go rockhounding with her boyfriend, Delmore), but once you got the knack of doing cabins, it wasn't really the worst way to spend a couple of hours. With any luck, Skinny Ribs would still be noodling around out there in the middle of Hadley Lake and she'd have the cabin to herself.

It was Hazel who'd shown her how to strip a bed, flip a mattress, put on new sheets so they fit as tight as the cover on a trampoline. Next, you poured disinfectant in the toilet bowl and let it do its thing while you tackled the vacuuming.

Vacuuming was kind of restful. Back and forth, back and forth, seven strokes each way, Hazel advised, all the while soothed by the roar of the ancient machine, which Gramma had threatened to replace with a slick new model out of the Sears catalog. Then a johnny mop was swished around the toilet bowl, fresh soap was laid in the soap dishes, and a stack of snowy towels was set on top of the commode. Once in a while, a grateful renter even left a dollar bill taped to the mirror or laid two quarters in one of the ashtrays.

Leenie wheeled her cart slowly down the cinder path toward cabin twelve. She wondered how old el weirdo was. Must be older than Sooz's brother, even if he didn't look like it, because he was traveling all over the country by himself. That'd mean he was at least twenty-two or three. Almost ready for Medicare. Older even than Mary Alice had been when—

Quit, Leenie, she told herself. Stop and desist. You promised not to think about that anymore.

Leenie tapped lightly on the door of cabin twelve. No answer came from inside. Whew; big relief. The dusty brown van was angle-parked beside the railroad ties that framed the cinder path; for sure he was out in the boat, still spying on sunbathers. What'd he think he was going to see that he'd never seen before, for heaven's sake?

She tried the door. It wasn't locked. She opened it a crack and peered in. The tiny kitchen, which had always reminded Leenie of the kitchen in a doll's house, seemed empty. A faint breeze teased the yellow curtains at the window above the sink. No sound came from deeper within the cabin. Leenie opened the door wider, stepped inside, and sucked in her breath.

A piece of plastic clothesline had been strung from the curtain rod above the sink to a handle on one of the cupboard doors across the room. Pinned onto it with colored clothespins were wet photographs in the process of drying. Newspapers had been spread neatly on the floor to catch the drips.

Now, one heartbeat at a time, Leenie understood: Skinny Ribs hadn't been looking at her with binoculars. He'd been studying her through the lens of a camera. Leenie peered at the images that had been hung to dry with a suffocated feeling in her chest.

There were lots of enlargements of a black-and-white cat sitting on the lid of a garbage can in the alley behind Quigley's Super-Valu in Wayburn. She recognized the spot right away because she used to take empty bottles to the back door of Quigley's to sell them for a nickel apiece.

Next came several shots of an old man sitting on a bench in a park Leenie didn't recognize. In each picture his expression was different, as if to reflect what was going on inside his head, but all of them were melancholy, even when there was a squirrel in the picture with him.

The last four pictures were of herself.

Gooseflesh leaped up on Leenie's arms and circled her neck like a collar. It wasn't fair. He'd had no right. Who gave him permission, anyway? But there she was, in a ratty old nightgown that was covered with faded pink unicorns . . . her feet were planted resolutely on the floor of the yellow lifeguard's tower . . . her hair was crazy and tangled from the sleepless night she'd just had . . . and the LIFEGUARD ON DUTY sign below her looked like a caption on a cartoon.

Had she really looked like that only three hours ago? Her expression was one Leenie didn't want to claim as her own. The face of the girl in the picture belonged to someone who was lost and lonely and bent on doing something goofy. Okay, maybe that *was* what she'd looked like; it was the principle of the thing that mattered. For a stranger to have captured all that on film—not once but four times!—was like, well, it was like—

"An invasion of privacy, right?" came a quiet voice behind Leenie. In all of Hazel's novels, the ones Leenie used to read in this very cabin, there was always a line that went "She whirled to face him, and her eyes blazed."

Leenie whirled, and tried to make her eyes blaze. She managed a feeble spark. "If you already know that, why'd you do it?" she demanded weakly. "I mean, who gave you permission? You just hauled off and—" She couldn't finish; it was all too humiliating.

Skinny Ribs was only a couple inches taller than she was herself. Not only were his eyes the color of gravel, they were the color of gravel after a summer rain, kind of gray-black and shiny. "I'm sorry if I offended you," he murmured. His voice was low and slow and deep. "I only had those four frames left to shoot," he explained, "and I was anxious to get the rest of the roll developed. I made a darkroom out of the bathroom; works pretty slick." It didn't seem to make him the least bit uncomfortable to look straight into her eyes.

Leenie glanced quickly away. He seemed to look through her and right out the other side. "It still doesn't seem fair," she insisted in a rusty voice.

"Sorry," he apologized again. Leenie could feel his glance search her face. She ducked her head so her tangled hair fell forward along her cheeks.

Then he must've decided the prints were dry enough to take down from the clothesline, for he began to collect them, and laid them in a pile on the counter of the snack bar. The four he'd taken of her were on the top.

"Actually, they're quite lovely," he observed. "There's no need for you to feel embarrassed at all."

Cautiously, Leenie examined the images. Rags of fog rose behind her and screened out all the cabins at the Dew Drop. Lucy McGee sat squarely at the base of the lifeguard's tower, her coat dark because it was wet. Lucy and I look like two characters about to embark on a mysterious journey, Leenie decided.

"You photograph very well," Skinny Ribs pointed out. "You have a kind of wild, leggy charm that is very attractive." Although she couldn't bring herself to look at him, Leenie felt the photographer smile at her reassuringly.

"Wild, leggy charm?" she echoed. That sure wasn't what Sooz had been saying lately. "Grow up, O'Brien," is what Sooz said. "You're not Huckleberry Finn, in case you haven't looked in the mirror lately. You're a girl, not a guy, a fact you can't seem to remember."

"It still doesn't seem fair," Leenie argued. "I was just sitting there, minding my own business, and now I feel—"

"Diminished, right? A little bit like a tribesman from New Guinea who believes his soul has been stolen if somebody takes his picture?"

"I don't know any tribesmen from New Guinea," Leenie squeaked. It was hard to recognize that high, thin voice as her own.

"Me, either," Skinny Ribs confessed. "I read that in a *National Geographic* once, that's all." Leenie allowed herself a quick glance at the photographer. His shiny, young-old eyes held hers easily.

"But I can see how upset you are," he told her as he gathered up the four photographs. "Here—you take these. My compliments. I'll even give you the negatives, if you'd like, so you can be sure I can't make any more prints." He selected four negatives from a plastic envelope and held them out to her. "Now—can we be friends?"

Friends? The possibility had never entered Leenie's mind. Nevertheless, she took the photographs and negatives. He must've taken her acceptance as an assent to friendship, she decided later, for he smiled genially and hopped onto one of the stools beside the snack bar. "My name's Axel Erickson," he told her, as if she really wanted to know.

"Axel? I never heard that name before. It's kind of weird."

"You wouldn't think so if you were named after your grandfather who came from Sweden where that name is quite common." He winked at her as easily as he had smiled, then folded his arms over his belt buckle. "Family history aside, I'm down here to take photos of Sawmill Swamp. You know anybody who could give me a guided tour of the place?"

Leenie moistened her lips and studied the air over the refrigerator. "Nope," she said quickly. "Actually, I don't know much about this place. I'm an orphan; I don't really belong here." Her inventiveness amazed her. "Besides, I hear that swamp is a dangerous place for strangers to go. There're all kinds of bad things that could happen to a person out there. I hear tell the trees out there are full of coachwhip snakes that hang down from the branches and sometimes drop right down the back of a person's neck."

"Gee, I'm sorry to hear that. That you're an orphan, I mean. I assumed maybe the man who rented this cabin to me was your dad and the lady with him was your moth—"

"That man's name is Jack O'Brien and the lady is the assistant manager here." True. "They're thinking about getting married." False. "They've been taking care of me for a while." True. "See, my folks were killed at a train crossing near Decatur five years ago and now Mr. O'Brien and Hazel have called a social worker to come and get me because they want to begin a happy life with just the two of them." False, false!

Leenie had never imagined that fibs could be as frisky as unicorns, but when Lucy McGee shoved her blonde head against the screen door, she listened to herself tell another one.

"That dog—I notice she's in your pictures, too—well, she's a champion. It's true. Won more blue ribbons than Gran—Mr. O'Brien, I mean—has room in his office to hang up. I suppose he could sell her for a thousand dollars if he wanted to." Maybe Lucy believed the story, too, Leenie marveled, because she settled herself on the porch outside with graceful pride.

Beyond Axel Erickson, on a table in the living room, Leenie spied a large photograph in a gold frame of a girl with pale, shiny hair. "Who's that?" she inquired, anxious to put some distance between herself and the yarns she'd just spun.

"Her name's Jane," Axel answered. Did she imagine it, Leenie wondered, or did he actually smile at the girl in the picture? "We've known each other a long time," he went on, "and after she's through gadding around the globe I expect we'll get married. Right now she's in England; she's writing a book about thatched cottages. Later this year I'll go over and take some pictures for her to illustrate it. She's fun to work with."

"No kidding." Leenie kept her voice vague and careful. Why did it pique her a little to hear that Axel Erickson knew a girl named Jane who looked as cool and pure as an aspirin and was fun to work with?

Axel clapped his hands on his knees and hopped down from his perch on the stool. "Well, if you don't know anything about Sawmill Swamp, I'll have to track down somebody who does," he said cheerfully. "I'm going to be doing a book about several swamps—the Great Dismal up in Virginia, the Okefenokee over in Georgia, the Everglades down in Florida—but I wanted to start with Sawmill because it's not as well-known and is kind of a small jewel in its own way."

Leenie swallowed. "Sorry I can't help you out," she muttered. "Guess I'm too shook up right now to even think of the name of anyone who could. That social worker I told you about is coming at the end of the month; I guess that's what's got me so upset. I hate to leave here, too, because these people have been awful good to me." She tried to imagine what it would be like to be deprived of the swamp, Lucy, Hazel, and Granda. She might as well be dead.

Leenie had allowed her right hand to rest idly on the counter of the snack bar. Axel Erickson reached out and covered her fingers with his own. "Listen," he said quietly, his gray-black glance searching her face again, "I know I can't help much, but if you ever want to rap about it—orphanhood, I mean—I'll be here till the end of the month."

Leenie hastily retrieved her fingers; his had left a warm track across her knuckles. "Oh, that's okay," she declared in a too-loud voice. "You know the old saying—the rainbow comes and goes." She smiled brightly and hoped she looked like a brave and plucky orphan. "Right now I better get started cleaning this place. It won't take long; I clean real quick." She opened the screen door, snatched some sheets and towels off the cart, and escaped into the bedroom of cabin twelve. Fibs made a person feel so peculiar, she decided; maybe she wouldn't tell any more for a long time.

Before she climbed into bed, Leenie taped the four photographic enlargements to the back of her bedroom door. She sat cross-legged on the end of her bed and studied them critically.

She had a wild and leggy charm, Axel Erickson had remarked. Wild and leggy, sure, but charm? Leenie peered intently at her own image but whatever charm was there escaped her. She was relieved, though, that none of her mosquito bites showed up. It was true, however, that her hair was as wild as a gypsy's, that her eyes were broody as a setting hen's.

Leenie shut off the lights and pulled the sheet up to her chin. But there was no way she could volunteer to guide Axel Erickson through the swamp. Sawmill Swamp and Sugar Island right in the middle of it, with its tiny ancient cabin she'd carefully furnished two years ago with peach crates and water buckets and bent silverware, were not places she intended to share with anyone.

5

Leenie lifted the dolls off the second shelf of her closet. Only one of them was even half cute: it was a soft, cloth doll that felt as sweet and squishy as the Pillsbury Doughboy looked on TV. There was still a single unopened box on the shelf; she took it down, too. Most of the packages that had arrived on birthdays and Easter had never been opened at all; she'd hauled them out to the garbage and burned them after writing insults all over their brown wrappers.

Leenie looked at the postmark on the unopened package that remained; it had arrived three years ago. She took a nail file from her dresser drawer and cut the tape that held the brown paper around the box. Inside was something covered with white tissue. A dumb blouse, probably.

Under the tissue was a pale blue sweater, size twelve, which was exactly what she'd been three years ago. With all her faults, at least Mary Alice could count.

The sweater was soft as a cloud under Leenie's fingers. The label read "90% Orlon, 10% Angora." No wonder it was so soft. Three years ago, when she'd been in eighth grade, sweaters like this one had been so popular and she'd wanted one so-o-o-o badly. Sooz had a peach-colored one (of course Sooz had everything, including two parents) and she wore it every Friday night when she went to the movies.

If I'd opened this package instead of writing insults all over it, I could've had a nifty sweater, too, Leenie realized.

A piece of folded paper had been tucked into one of the sleeves of the sweater and fell out when Leenie held the sweater up to herself to look at it in the mirror. The writing on it was the same graceful kind that'd been on the vanilla envelope. She read with suspicious eyes.

"When I saw this sweater, Arlene, I thought right away of you. Someone I know—I'm sure you'd like him if you ever had a chance to meet him—told me this shade of blue made him think of a faded dream. I thought those words sounded like they'd come right out of a poem! Well, Arlene, I hope that you have a very happy birthday. Love, Your Mother."

Leenie folded the sweater quickly and stuck it back into the box. She clamped the lid on so that she wouldn't have to look at it. I don't have a mother, she wanted to inform Mary Alice. What Sooz has is a mother; what I have is somebody who got pregnant by mistake, then had to have a baby. There's a difference, lady, in case you never noticed. And that stuff about faded dreams—so much baloney. Leenie tried to decide whether or not to burn the sweater. Well, maybe not. Hazel's niece Bitsie was twelve now; she could probably get some good out of it.

Leenie wandered into the kitchen. The Big Cabin seemed as big as a barracks with both Hazel and Granda gone. Hazel's car had turned out to be a lemon, so Granda had gone back to Decatur with Hazel to see if the used-car warranty meant Hazel could trade Agnes for a car that really ran. Right away he'd named Hazel's car Agnes Abercrombie, but that hadn't kept the poor old lady from wheezing a lot and having to lean up against the roadside to rest every few miles.

Leenie drifted into Granda's office. Before it was an office it'd been a sunporch that overlooked the lake. Now it held a desk, two filing cabinets, and a bookcase. Leenie settled herself behind the desk and hoped a couple of tourist families would show up. She'd take down their names and addresses and ask for the license numbers of their cars. If the first family to arrive had three kids, she'd put them in cabin six, which was large and had been empty for two weeks; if the second family had two kids, they could have cabin three, which had been vacated only yesterday.

She stared moodily through the window and across the water. Axel Erickson was out in the middle of the lake again. Fortunately, most days he left the Dew Drop early in the morning and was gone all day. She wondered if he was still looking for someone to guide him into the swamp. Or maybe he spent his days taking more pictures of cats on garbage cans. Leenie was glad when she saw him leave every day; otherwise she'd have to worry about running into him accidentally. The second time Eloise called in sick, she'd had to trade cabins real quick with Hazel.

"What's the matter?" Hazel wanted to know. "That young dude from New York come on to you? He'd darn well better pick somebody closer to his own age, if you want my personal opinion."

"When I do, I'll let you know." Leenie yawned and tried to look casual. "Not that you have to worry—he's all set to marry a girl named Jane, not to mention he's hardly my type."

"Seems to me you don't exactly have a type," Hazel had observed.

Maybe I don't intend to, Leenie wanted to reply. Just look what happened to Mary Alice; you think I want to end up like that? Forget it. The thing was, if a person fell in love—to say "fell in love" made it sound like an accident had happened, like falling off a dock, maybe—then a person might get pregnant, have a kid she didn't want, have to dump it on someone else.

Leenie checked her watch. Only ten minutes had passed. She peeled a sheet off Granda's notepad and made a few notes to herself.

1. Remember to give Luce her cod-liver oil tonight! Also, don't forget her worm medicine!!!
2. Refill all the Glass-B-Brite bottles in the shed.
3. Call Sooz and see if she wants to go to a movie tonight.

Leenie studied the list. Might as well call Sooz right now, she decided. She pulled the phone closer and dialed Sooz's number, which was as familiar as her own.

"Sooz? It's me. Hey, let's go to that movie at the Imago tonight. It's about these two people, see, who have a curse put on them by a wizard, so the girl has to be a hawk by day and the guy turns into a wolf at night, which means they never get to—"

An agonized groan on the other end of the line made Leenie hold the phone away from her ear. "You got any idea what time it is, Leen?" Sooz complained loudly. "It's only ten o'clock and you know for a fact I never get up until noon! Besides"—she paused and yawned mightily—"I already saw it. Last night. I went with Chuckie Bedell."

"You went to a movie with Chuckie Bedell?"

"Yeah." This time, Sooz's yawn was small and pleased. "He finally succumbed to my fatal charms."

You mean he tripped when you stuck your foot out, Leenie thought. Sooz had acted like a total lunatic over Chuckie all summer. But why? She and Sooz had known Chuckie since first grade. How come he was all of a sudden special? Okay, so he'd gotten a lot taller. So his mom helped him bleach his hair and gave him a perm so it was curly all over. So it looked kind of cute. So he played defensive end for the Wayburn Warriors last year when they won their first All-Conference title. So what? How could a guy you'd both known all your lives be anything except a guy you'd known all your lives?

"The thing about you, Leen, is you're still hung up on your dumb boat, that swamp, all that old nature-girl business," Sooz said. "I, on the other hand, have moved on to bigger and better things. Namely, Chuckie Bedell."

"You used to like to come out here for overnights," Leenie accused. "You thought it was fun to jump in the *Swamp Rat* and go catch some bluegills or a few silversides."

"That was before, Leen."

"Before what?"

"Before Chuckie, dopus." There was a muffled sound from Sooz and Leenie knew she was pulling the sheet over her head to keep the sun out of her eyes and had dragged the phone into the sheet tent with her.

"Now what I'm going to lay on you is for your own good, Leen," Sooz counseled. Sure, Leenie thought, just like you'd give me a five-year diary if you found out I had six months to live. "See, Leen, you want to keep right on doing the same old stuff we did when we were kids. Only I'm different now. Chuckie's a neat guy; he's got a great bod and he kisses super. To be honest, Leen, I think I've got the urge to merge."

Leenie rested the phone in its cradle without bothering to say good-bye. The urge to merge—how could anyone be so stupid? she wondered with disgust. Not that she hadn't seen it coming with her own eyes: Sooz wore mascara and eye shadow all the time, even when she wasn't going anywhere special, and the bathing suit she got this summer wasn't much bigger than some of the ones on the tourists' little kids.

"He's got a great bod," Leenie repeated in a garpy voice. "He kisses super!" She gagged again. Lucy, sleeping under Granda's desk, stirred in alarm. Leenie buried her toes in Lucy's thick fur to quiet her and tried to imagine what school would be like in September. The pits, that's what it'd be like.

There wouldn't be anybody to walk around the halls with because Sooz would be hanging out with Chuckie all the time, just like Angela Nelson did last year with that gross Jason Bates. Between classes, Sooz and Chuckie would lean against their lockers, stare meaningfully into one another's eyes, and give each other mouth-to-mouth resuscitation. Who could imagine what they did when they were alone? I'll have to join the Booster Club, get on the school paper, do something important so I won't have to watch them, Leenie decided. She made another garpy sound, which caused Lucy to scramble from under the desk, ready to administer assistance in case the emergency got worse.

Leenie reached absentmindedly to smooth Lucy's ears. Overhead, the fan stirred the air in warm, lazy waves. I won't think about Sooz or Chuckie anymore, she promised herself. Thinking about those two only made her feel more wounded than ever.

Trouble was, though, it seemed like she was populating a whole country in her head with people she didn't want to think about. Mary Alice. Axel Erickson. Now Sooz and Chuckie, too. It was like she could only feel happy if she pretended that none of them mattered.

Clean up your act, Leenie, she told herself. She'd start by finding something to read until Granda and Hazel showed up. That way she'd also look efficient and businesslike in case any tourists came by.

Leenie peered at Granda's bookcase. *Small Business Management;* boy, he'd read that one until it was limp. *Guide to the Great Swamps of America;* he used to read parts of that one to her instead of a regular bedtime story. Next to the swamp book was a small one she didn't recognize. The legend on its spine was blurry and hard to make out. She lifted it off the shelf. *The Wayburn High School Annual,* Leenie read.

When Mary Alice left so long ago, Gramma had banished every picture, each memento, all tangible evidences of her daughter from the house, a fact Leenie might not have been sure about except that Hazel told her it was so.

"Your Gramma always treated *me* right," Hazel admitted. "She paid me what was due me and she paid me on time—but with her own family, she was an unforgiving old bird. Things would've been easier if she'd lightened up a little—I mean, Mary Alice wasn't the first girl in the world who ever got pregnant without getting married first. Things didn't necessarily have to turn out the way they did."

"The way they did?" Leenie had echoed.

"Making Mary Alice feel so bad and humiliated she'd ten times rather live eight hundred miles from Wayburn is what I mean," Hazel had explained.

Leenie opened the book slowly. Somehow or another, this solitary memento had escaped Gramma's wrath. Granda must've slid it between the *Small Business Management* guide and his book about the great swamps, and for sixteen years it'd been right here at his fingertips. How many times had he looked at it and lamented the fate of his only daughter?

The photographs of all the graduating seniors were right at the front of the annual. Not that Mary Alice actually graduated in a cap and gown with everybody else; she'd had to leave school three months early, had to finish her class work at home where nobody could see her disgrace.

"Big as a barn when all her friends were like reeds," Leenie had overheard Gramma hiss at Granda one day. Leenie couldn't remember what Granda had murmured in reply. Nothing, probably. In lots of ways, he was just as soft and sweet as that doll in the closet, the one that looked like the Pillsbury Doughboy.

The pictures of the Wayburn seniors were only about one inch square, hardly enough of a picture to tell much about a person you'd never met. Only three kids had names starting with O, and Mary Alice came first. Leenie got the magnifying glass out of Granda's desk drawer, the one he used to read maps, and inspected the face of the person whose image was suddenly enlarged before her.

Mary Alice's light-brown hair was parted in the middle and hung down, plain and straight, till it touched the collar of her white blouse. Her eyes looked steadily past Leenie into a future that only she could see. Mary Alice's full lips didn't smile but they didn't frown, either. She looked a lot like Granda, Leenie realized with surprise—quiet and steady and sweet.

I've missed her, Leenie realized. I thought I couldn't, because I don't even know her. But I've missed her. Always.

Slowly, Leenie turned the other pages. The boys and girls who stared back at her were grown men and women now. There was a picture of Sooz's mom; she'd been pretty once. And one of these guys might be my father, Leenie mused. Which one? She peered through the magnifying glass at a boy with freckles. No, not him. A boy with curly blond hair came next. No, not him, either. Who, then? Or would she ever know?

She'd never let on to Gramma, of course, but once she'd found her birth certificate. Gramma kept it, of all places, in a drawer in the kitchen underneath all the recipes she clipped out of the newspaper and then never looked at again. Mother: Mary Alice O'Brien, age 17, the certificate informed Leenie. Father: Unknown.

Lucy, satisfied that Leenie had recovered from her attack of nausea, slid onto the floor beside the door and went back to sleep. Leenie glanced out the window; Axel Erickson must've rowed back to shore because the lake was deserted now.

That birth certificate is another thing I don't like to think too much about, Leenie realized. It would've been easier to have had a dad who died in Vietnam, like Chuckie Bedell's. At least Chuckie knew who his dad was and where he was. If a person had a Father Unknown, he just kind of floated around out there in space, faceless and nameless, neither tall nor short nor thin nor fat nor much of anything at all.

Leenie closed the *Wayburn High School Annual* and put it back on the bookshelf. She smoothed her right index finger along the inside of her elbow. She peered at the fine dark hairs on her arm, at the mole on her knuckle. Maybe that mole was like one Mary Alice had. And my eyes—Gramma said they were the color of cold coffee—but maybe they're exactly like my father's. Only I don't know for sure because both of them dumped me. I might as well have white hair and pink eyes and be called Harold for all those two cared.

Leenie took another piece of paper from Granda's rainbow-colored notepad. She would be judge and jury. She drew a line down the middle of the paper, wrote Mary Alice's name on one side and Father Unknown on the other. Today, guilt would be assigned as it was so richly deserved.

Mary Alice got an X right away because Leenie heard Gramma tell Hazel once that smart girls didn't do what Mary Alice had done. She got a second X because Sooz reported that her mother said a girl could make a boy behave if she really wanted to.

But there was always rape. Leenie paused. She'd thought about that a lot. All you had to do was read the newspaper or watch TV to know stuff like that happened all the time. It might've happened to Mary Alice. Maybe this guy, Father Unknown, had kind of kidnapped her and held a knife to her throat and threatened to do something even worse if she ever told what'd happened.

What if Mary Alice went to him later and said, "I'm pregnant. I'm going to have a baby." He might've gotten out his knife again and said, "You tell anybody it's me who's the father of that kid and I'll get rid of both of you." Such a dreadful threat might've driven Mary Alice out of town and kept her silent for sixteen years. It was possible. Leenie's suspicions made her give Father Unknown two large Xs on his side and take one back from Mary Alice.

Leenie folded the paper in half again and put it in her hip pocket. It wasn't much fun being a judge and jury. *Judge:* This woman and this man have been accused of abandoning their child. *Jury:* We hereby find them both guilty and recommend a life sentence with no parole. Maybe a life sentence was too long; just the same, she hoped they'd both suffered plenty.

A hiss of airbrakes sounded on the road outside. Lucy McGee roused herself, stretched, and yawned. It was probably the rural bus, letting Hazel off. Hey, wait, Leenie thought. Hazel was with Granda; they'd gone in their cars, not on the bus. Sometimes, though, weekenders came out on the bus from Wayburn. Leenie left Granda's desk and went to the door.

Someone was standing in a cloud of pinkish dust that was already beginning to settle back onto the road in front of the Dew Drop. A tall someone who seemed vaguely familiar and who wore a pale lavender suit about the color of the amethyst ring Sooz got for her birthday last year. The woman had long legs and wore strappy little shoes on her narrow feet. A brown leather handbag was slung over her left shoulder and a suitcase the same color rested in the road beside her. Her light, shiny hair hung even with her suit collar, and her full lips neither smiled nor frowned.

I hate her, Leenie reminded herself. Besides, she's not supposed to be here for another week. There's no way I can ever like her because she dumped me when I was only three months old and I hope she's gone to sleep every single night regretting the terrible mistake she made. Truthfully, though, the woman standing in the road didn't look as if her life had been a sentence in Pitsville without hope of parole. Something worse occurred to Leenie: *What if I can't keep on hating her?*

It definitely would've been easier to do if Mary Alice looked the way she was supposed to look. Wild and hard. Decorated with cheap jewelry that left green rings around her neck and wrists and fingers. Wearing so much eye makeup she looked like somebody's pet raccoon. The woman standing in the road didn't have on any jewelry and wore no more makeup than Hazel. She was so overall ordinary it was a disappointment.

But she doesn't see me yet, Leenie realized. Which means I still have time to sneak out the back door. I could push the *Swamp Rat* into the water, jump into it, and head straight for Sugar Island. I could stay there until I was pretty sure she was gone.

There was another alternative, of course. I could stick around awhile, Leenie admitted to herself. I could give her maybe twenty-four hours to explain to me why she dumped me, why she never came back, why she let my grandparents raise me up for sixteen years even though she knew for a fact my grandmother wasn't going to like me very much, considering how I got here. I could do that. If I wanted to.

Leenie opened the screen door and stepped out of the office.

"Hello, Mary Alice," she said. There was one thing she probably couldn't ever do, though, no matter how good her intentions were. She probably could never call Mary Alice *Mother.*

Mary Alice didn't say anything right away. After a minute, she left her suitcase in the middle of the road and walked slowly forward. She stopped about ten feet away. When she smiled, Leenie saw that she had quirky eyeteeth, just like Granda, and a dimple in her left cheek.

"Hello, Arlene," she answered softly. "You look exactly like I always dreamed you would."

6

It was Hazel, the last person in the world Leenie would've suspected of such treachery, who right away started to behave like a complete and total fool.

"Let me have a look at you, honeybun!" she cried the minute she laid eyes on Mary Alice. Leenie had just finished making a pot of Orange Mist tea and had set out two blue cups and a plate of store-bought cookies when old busybody Hazel waded right in and ruined everything.

"My, don't you look just good enough to kiss!" Hazel squealed. Taking her own suggestion, she seized Mary Alice in her brown arms and planted several moist, noisy kisses all over the poor woman's face.

Can you believe that nitwit? Leenie marveled, and was careful to pretend that tea and cookies with Mary Alice didn't matter any more than a movie with Sooz had. Why did I ever think I wanted Granda to marry such an idiot? Leenie asked herself. Only this morning it was *me* she was calling honeybun; now here she is, falling all over Mary Alice like a big blue whale.

That's exactly what Hazel looked like, too, a huge blue whale in that pair of jeans that must be at least size 20 and that shirt a person could've made a small tent out of. If certain people lost a few pounds, then certain people wouldn't have to cut holes in the sides of their new tennies, either.

Mary Alice, Leenie noted sourly, did not seem to be paying much attention to any of Hazel's faults. In fact, it looked as if she was hugging and kissing Hazel right back. *Dis*gusting! Leenie crossed her arms over her chest and gave herself a squeeze. Might as well, she decided; nobody else seemed to want to.

And the look that came across Granda's face was no improvement over the goofy one pasted all over Hazel's. He looked happy. Not pretend happy, but *happy*, like something had just happened that he'd been waiting for forever. As soon as Hazel let loose of Mary Alice, he had to have his turn, of course. He was a little more discreet: he simply lifted each of Mary Alice's pretty hands in his own big ones and held her at arm's length.

"Oh, girl, you just look so *fine*," he whispered. The word *fine* sounded even better than a hug. "I just wish it hadn't taken you sixteen long years to come home again."

"Oh, Daddy, you know the old saying, 'You can't go home again,' " Mary Alice began in a chokey voice. Her eyes gleamed with tears but she didn't cry. Doesn't want to make her eyes red, Leenie suspected. "Well, for a long time I really believed that was true," Mary Alice went on. "I was so ashamed, knowing how Momma always felt about what I did. But things change; people do, too. I knew I couldn't live the rest of my life without coming home at least once."

Your first idea was your best one, Leenie wanted to advise. It would've been better if you'd stayed away. And that infernal Daddy and Momma stuff—Leenie did some quick arithmetic: if Mary Alice was seventeen when I was born, she calculated, and I'm sixteen now, that means she's thirty-three years old. Way too old for names like Daddy and Momma. I guess I'll be able to hate her pretty easy after all, she decided.

Hazel galloped over to the refrigerator, her holey tennies squeaking cheerfully on the clean floor, and hauled out a dish of chicken wings that had been marinating since early morning in a special soy sauce recipe. Ordinarily, Leenie loved Hazel's oriental chicken wings better than Lucy liked rib bones, but tonight might be an exception.

"Remember these, sweet thing?" Hazel crooned and stuck the dish under Mary Alice's nose. "I brought these to a picnic once when you were only about twelve, way back when I still had my poor Jeffie with me. My, how you loved old Hazel's chicken wings!"

And I was dumb enough to think old Hazel was merely a whale, Leenie railed privately. I was wrong; she's a black-hearted traitor, that's what she really is. She's all ready to welcome Mary Alice back without a single word of reproach. Let bygones be bygones, right? Wrong. I'll forgive her on the twelfth of never, Leenie thought, but not a single day sooner.

"It was fate, Hazel," Mary Alice cooed back across the dish of chicken wings. "You didn't even know for sure exactly when I'd be here but you had your famous chicken wings all ready for me!"

La dee dah. Compliments were flying around the kitchen faster than unguided ballistic missiles. Smiles were flashing on and off like neon signs. Leenie squandered another hug on herself. Even with the air conditioning off, she felt strangely cool.

At dinner, Hazel and Mary Alice commenced to talk about people Leenie had never heard of in her life. "Did you hear sweet little Becky Reynolds had twins?" Hazel mumbled around a mouthful of chicken. "She married that nice Thaxter boy, you know, the one who got that big scholarship to the university. And Madge Crane? Red hair, tall, freckles? Well, she's been married twice; had four nice kids now, two girls by one husband and two boys by the other."

"And what ever happened to Josie Sharp?" Mary Alice was dying to know. "Or Roger Barry? Remember Roger? He was the one who—"

Leenie quit listening. What had Hazel done to her dumb old chicken wings? They tasted terrible. Those other three hadn't noticed yet; they were pigging out on chicken wings and potato salad and fresh tomatoes as if food rationing started tomorrow. Leenie studied them bitterly: Hazel was flushed and pink as a watermelon right through her suntan. . . . Granda was laughing even though nobody'd said anything funny. . . . Mary Alice's honey-colored hair swung like a shiny curtain against her cheeks when she turned from Hazel to Granda and back to Hazel again.

The truth dawned slowly on Leenie. *I'm the one who doesn't matter anymore,* she realized. I'm the one who doesn't count now.

Why had it taken her so long to understand? Leenie asked herself. All the time Granda had been raising her, buying her a dog, building her a boat, teaching her about the swamp—all that time, he'd just been waiting for the day Mary Alice would come back so life could go on the way it was supposed to.

For the first time ever, Leenie felt a bond with Gramma. Sure, she was a tough old bird, just like Hazel said she was, but nobody ever said she was a fool. She wouldn't have been tricked into believing Mary Alice had changed. After all, didn't Mary Alice know a guy now who thought the color blue was like a faded dream? No doubt she'd run off with him next. So why pretend to be a real family? We aren't, Leenie realized. We are four separate people, each one going a different direction.

"'Scuse me, please," Leenie murmured politely. Speaking of directions, she knew for sure where she was headed. "I don't feel so hot," she murmured, and kept her voice cool. She studied the chicken bones on her plate. "What'd you put in the sauce this time, Hazel?" she accused softly. "Those wings were kind of yukky."

Hazel didn't look as abashed as Leenie had hoped she would. "You guys go right ahead with your visit," she heard herself say, "while I go lie down for a little while, okay?" The three of them nodded, only slightly perplexed. Leenie decided they probably didn't care a whit one way or the other.

"Now that you mention it, sweet pea, you do look a mite green around the gills," Hazel had enough sense to admit finally. "Maybe I ought to come with you and—"

"It's no big deal," Leenie insisted smoothly. She started down the hall to her room but paused long enough beyond the kitchen door to get the drift of their conversation once they figured she was out of earshot.

"Let's face it," she heard Hazel suggest, "it's been an awful shock for her. It isn't every day a sixteen-year-old girl meets her mother for the very first time, you know."

"You're right," Mary Alice sighed, "but I hope I can help her understand that I never left because I didn't love her. It's just that I can't turn back the clock and undo what I did."

Turning back the clock is not the problem, Leenie wanted to inform her. The problem is, you came back. Nobody asked you to, not even Granda. I never wrote you a letter, never played with your stupid dolls, never wore your dumb blue sweater, either.

"But you're not the only parent she had," Leenie heard Granda murmur. "Her daddy has some stake in this, too." Oh, you mean old Father Unknown? Leenie wanted to call into the kitchen. How can he have a stake in anything, considering he didn't even want his name on my birth certificate? She decided she'd heard more than enough and hurried down the hall to her room and shut the door.

Leenie reached under her bed and pulled out her backpack and sleeping bag. They'd been ready for two weeks, ever since Mary Alice's letter arrived. In the pack were five pounds of dry dog food, four cans of tuna fish, a large jar of peanut butter, some instant coffee, and as many cans of raspberry soda as could be squeezed in around everything else. A flashlight, matches, soap, and two towels were already waiting under one of the benches in the *Swamp Rat*.

Leenie opened her bedroom window as wide as it would go, dropped her stuff out, and climbed through after it. Lucy McGee was lying at the corner of the Big Cabin in the middle of a bed of nasturtiums that Hazel had planted in the spring.

"Get your rear in gear," Leenie advised. The words electrified Lucy, who rose out of the flower bed like she was on fire and headed straight for the dock. I swear that dog is twice as smart as a lot of people I know, Leenie thought. When those three back there in the kitchen got up in the morning, they'd probably be real puzzled to discover that she was gone. Later, they'd begin to worry. Good.

Revenge tasted a lot like limeade, Leenie decided, a little sweet but a little sour, too. The trouble was, Granda was sixty-three years old. What if her disappearance gave him a heart attack or something? She paused and pulled a piece of paper out of her hip pocket. It was the list of sins she'd attributed to Mary Alice and Father Unknown. Leenie took the felt pen from her other pocket, scribbled through the Xs, blacked out her parents' names, then turned the paper to its clean side.

"*Granda,*" she wrote, dispensing with the pleasantry of Dear, "*Lucy and I are going out to Sugar Island for a few days. I'm taking plenty to eat and I'll probably catch lots of fish. Don't worry about me. Love, L.*" She hesitated, then added, "*P.S. Please tell Mary Alice good-bye. It was nice to meet her, but there's no sense her hanging around until I get back.*"

Leenie rolled the note into a tube and poked it through a link in one of the chains that held the lifeguard's sign on the tower. Granda would come down here about nine o'clock tomorrow morning and would find her message even before he'd had a chance to be upset.

Lucy McGee was already in the boat and had taken her usual position in the prow. Leenie tossed her gear in, stripped off her tennies, and rolled her jeans up to her knees. The soft, wet sand squeezed coolly between her toes as she loosened her tie-up rope and pushed off. The punt pole lay in the bottom of the boat; she wouldn't need to use it until she got closer to the swamp. Three feet from shore, Leenie jumped into the *Swamp Rat,* took her paddles out of their locks, and began to row.

Axel Erickson had sure looked silly that morning as he chopped at the lake as if it were frozen, she reflected. By comparison, just look how the *Swamp*

Rat moved—as silently as a dream. Leenie breathed deeply and pulled against the water. One at a time, those three back there in the Big Cabin fell out of her mind, as she'd known they would. A familiar feeling took hold of her, as it always did when she was on her way to Sugar Island. Out there, with Lucy McGee as her only companion, the word illegitimate didn't mean anything at all. Out there, a person could just be.

7

Leenie glanced over her shoulder. Squares of orange light winked cozily in most of the Little Cabins. Number twelve, she noticed, was dark.

But the picture window in the living room of the Big Cabin glowed like a beacon in the falling darkness. Hazel had made a pecan pie before she went off with Granda to trade Agnes Abercrombie for a car that ran; now she and Granda and Mary Alice were probably watching TV and talking and having pie with their coffee. The pie wouldn't be much good, though, Leenie thought with grim satisfaction. Hazel had probably wrecked it just like she goofed up on her chicken wings.

Leenie turned her back on the distant shore and concentrated on rowing. Life was weird, she decided. When you were little, most days were just great, even when you had a Gramma who was grouchy. Then one day your best friend walked up to you and told you that you were illegitimate and after that, nothing was the same. At first, you pretended it didn't matter; by the time you got in junior high you knew it did. When you were about to start eleventh grade, you thought about it practically every day.

Leenie rested her oars in their locks and picked up a spray can of Bug-Off from the floor of the boat.

She gave herself a couple blasts from it. Some years, mosquitos around the swamp were like jumbo jets, other years like Piper Cubs. This year was a Piper Cub year. She dropped the spray can back into her pack.

It had never occurred to her to wonder about it before—had Mary Alice liked the swamp, too? Granda'd never mentioned one way or the other. Leenie reflected on what Mary Alice had looked like as she stood in the road: slim, pretty in a scrubbed and ordinary way, wearing a suit the color of Sooz's amethyst ring. Naw. She didn't look like a person who'd care beans about a swamp. Just one more thing that made them totally different from one another.

Leenie began to row again. And I'm lots different from Sooz, too, she mused. Sooz was giving Chuckie a rush now, which was dumb, since she knew him as well as she knew her own brother. Chuckie had been so chubby in sixth grade; then his plumpness seemed to move around so now he had big shoulders and a cute tush but no fat anywhere else. Once, in a fit of madness that had lasted about two weeks, Leenie had imagined what it might be like if she and Chuckie ever—but luckily, that craziness passed and she realized it was stupid to get romantic about anybody, least of all a guy she'd known since first grade.

The Swamp Rat slid silently through the clear water. One interesting thing about Chuckie, though: not having a dad didn't seem to bother him much. Well, in a way, he had one now; his mom got married again three years ago to a guy who sold cars for the Buick dealer in Wayburn and who always drove a nice demonstrator model that, on rare occasions, Chuckie got to drive himself. Chuckie even got two stepsisters, Marie and June, in the deal, so now he belonged to a more-or-less regular family.

Leenie let her oars drag in the water and lifted a large jar of peanut butter out of her pack. She dug a glob out with her finger and plastered it to the roof of her mouth. When she was nine or ten, she reflected, she'd stick the peanut butter up behind her front teeth and run her tongue back and forth over it until it was all gone. Sometimes she wished she'd never grown up. When you were little, all it took to make you happy was a glob of peanut butter stuck behind your front teeth.

Lucy McGee gave Leenie an impatient let's-get-moving look from the prow of the boat. "Okay, okay, I'm coming!" Leenie muttered.

When a person got older, life was different in lots of unexpected ways. For one thing, you lost the body you'd spent about twelve years getting used to. Leenie fondly remembered her old one: it'd been skinny as spaghetti, with a bone on each hip that nicely held up a pair of jeans, had shoulders as high and square as Chuckie Bedell's, though naturally not as brawny. The body she got in its place had lumps and bumps and humps in places that once had been sleek as an otter's. The disappearance of that old self made Leenie feel mournful, like somebody she knew real well had just died.

Well, maybe somebody had, she mused. Maybe that careless, skinny old Leenie just crawled off somewhere and had breathed her last.

The uncluttered water of Hadley Lake began to change character beneath the *Swamp Rat*. Now, the water that flowed past the boat seemed dirty. Leenie knew it wasn't really; it was only that the accumulated detritis of the swamp—bits of bark, grass, leaves, and chunks of peat from the swamp floor, which were all acidic—had stained the water the color of dark tea.

An hour later, Leenie drew abreast of what looked to be an impenetrable wall of straw-colored maiden cane grass. She knew that if she grabbed some of that grass, bent it over into the boat, and shook it, tiny frogs, beetles, even a baby snake or two would fall out of it. Old-time swampers used to shake maiden cane into their boats and use its harvest for bait on their fish lines; long ago, Granda had showed her how to do the same.

Leenie eased the *Swamp Rat* along the grass wall, whose roots were fastened on the swamp floor, and nosed the boat into what seemed to be a narrow canal. She laid her oars in their locks and reached for the punt pole. She stood up, braced her feet wide, and began to pole, pressing the tip of the pole against the peaty floor of the swamp so the boat scooted forward. Poling was like vacuuming, Leenie thought; while you did it, your mind kind of emptied itself of all its troubles.

She felt the muscles of her arms, back, and thighs strain easily against the pole. Soon a light sweat dampened her underarms and the sleek new hollow between her breasts. Breasts—for a while she wondered which would be worse, to get them or not to get them. That part of growing up had happened so fast; one day she was just a skinny kid, the next day she woke up to find out she'd turned into someone she'd never intended to be.

Not Sooz, though. Sooz thought her new body was great. When she got her first period, you'd have thought she had just invented the light bulb. "Now I'm like my mom and my sister Clarice!" she'd breathed, actually glad about the whole business.

Maybe that's why I'm not, Leenie reflected. Maybe I'm scared that now I could turn into someone just like Mary Alice. Horrible thought.

Leenie checked her watch. The neat thing about digitals was that no matter how dark it got, you could still see the numbers. Nine-thirty; she was making good time. She glanced back, thinking she might get a final glimpse of the Dew Drop's cabins, but the wall of maiden cane screened the far shore from view. On her right, Leenie noticed low, dark clouds scudding swiftly behind a row of brooding cypress trees. A storm was moving in from the coast, she realized. They could come up quickly this time of year, but this one seemed to be coming faster than usual.

Lucy sensed a storm was coming, too, and left her post at the prow to come back midships and rest her haunches against Leenie's bare foot. "Chicken," Leenie accused softly. No matter how many blows they'd been through together, Lucy never resigned herself to any of them.

Leenie paused. Should she make a run for Sugar Island? She wetted her lips with her tongue. No, it was too far away; she'd never make it. She'd better tie up quick, ride out the storm, travel on after it'd worn itself out.

Now the sky to the east was black and the air had cooled ominously. The Atlantic Ocean, which broke against the coast, was only forty miles away. It took only minutes for a big blow to get inland when it was powered by winds of eighty to a hundred miles an hour.

Except I do have one other option, Leenie realized. I could turn back. But what had Mary Alice said before supper? "You can't go home again," that's what she'd said. Well, I can't either, Leenie told herself. She turned the nose of the *Swamp Rat* toward the cypress grove two hundred yards away and poled hard.

Sooz thought cypresses were kind of gross, with their enormous, twisted roots reaching out of the water as they did. "They're cousins of the redwoods, and people drive out to California to see those all the time," Leenie had pointed out. Right now, the important thing was that cypress trees rarely went down in a storm because their wide, fluted bases were anchored firmly to the peat floor of the swamp by roots that reached laterally in many directions, like spokes from a wheel.

Leenie threw her tie-up rope around a cypress knee, a knobby, hollow protuberance that grew upward from a submerged tree root. Sooz called them warts and said they were ugly, but Granda had explained that knees helped to aerate the waterlogged tree roots and were one of the reasons a cypress could live to be three or four hundred years old.

When the rain started, it plinked down softly in drops as big as quarters on the black surface of the water. Five minutes later, it splattered everywhere like bullets from a machine gun. Lucy laid her ears flat and dove under one of the seats in the center of the boat. Leenie snatched her tarpaulin off the floor of the *Swamp Rat*, fastened it quickly to each side of the boat with elastic shock cord, and crawled under it to lie beside Lucy.

The dog buried her blonde head in Leenie's armpit. "Poor old 'fraidy cat," Leenie soothed. "We'll just ride 'er out, like we always do, okay?" Lucy raised her head long enough to wet Leenie's cheek with her tongue. Leenie smiled ruefully in the darkness. Chuckie kisses Sooz; my dog kisses me. Some romance.

* * *

When Leenie woke, the *Swamp Rat* was rocking quietly on the water and there was no sound of bullets ricocheting off the tarp. Leenie peered at her watch. Twelve-thirty. A silver blade of moonlight pierced a worn spot in the canvas over her heart. She unsnapped the shock-cord tie-downs at the sides of the *Swamp Rat* and peered out.

The water all around was black as oil. Moonlight glinted off its surface, which was pocked by tiny waves that hadn't yet subsided from the wind. The tangle of holly and fetterbush that clogged the entrance to the cypress bay was tarnished silver in the moonlight. Ghostly curtains of Spanish moss, pale as platinum, hung from the branches of the cypress tree above. The last of the storm clouds were scudding up the coast toward Savannah. It was safe to go now.

Leenie folded the tarp while Lucy stretched and yawned as if the ordeal hadn't concerned her at all. The air was cool, but the water was still warm from a full day of sun so now mist rose off its dimpled surface like silver smoke. Leenie untied the *Swamp Rat* and pushed the boat away from the shelter of the cypress grove.

When Leenie came to a dead cypress silhouetted against the indigo sky, she turned sharply left. As she did, something pale drifted past, carried by the current of one of the many freshwater creeks that fed the swamp. She squinted hard. A log? An abandoned boat? It wasn't exactly white; gray or green, maybe. As it drifted off into the dappled shadows, she was sure she saw something painted on it. A number? Couldn't be, she decided. Her nerves must be playing tricks on her.

Twenty minutes later, Leenie could see the tin roof of the cabin on Sugar Island gleaming dully in the silver light. She paused. No, it was an owl, not a human voice she'd just heard. The only other sounds that came to her ears were the music of the frogs, the wind in the trees, the light tattoo of her own heart.

She nosed the *Swamp Rat* into the reeds that grew thickly at the edge of the island. The old dock, built by folks who'd lived here long before Granda's time, had rotted away, so she had to pole the punt until it grounded itself in the soft muck beyond the reeds. She rolled up her pants legs again, hoisted her pack and sleeping bag, and, with the tie-up rope looped over her arm, eased herself into the water. Lucy, her confidence in Mother Nature restored, leaped noisily overboard and sloshed happily toward high ground.

When she got to high ground herself, Leenie looked for a familiar stump and fastened her rope to it. Granda had never been sure who'd built the one-room cabin on the island; maybe it'd been a Civil War deserter, he'd said. That would make it well over a hundred years old, but since it'd been built of cypress wood, it might last forever. Whoever had come here so long ago had also brought a magnolia tree and had planted it beside the porch. Soon Leenie could see its familiar, waxy blooms glowing like lamps in the shadow of the tin roof.

Lucy caught the scent of a rabbit and went slamming off into the tangle of shrubs beyond the cabin. Old Luce knows she's home same as I do, Leenie thought as she picked her way up the overgrown path toward the porch. Moonlight lit the front of the cabin like a street lamp. Leenie caught herself in midstride as she was about to mount the bottom step.

The door of the cabin was slightly ajar.

She distinctly remembered closing it the last time she was on Sugar Island. But that'd been two whole months ago. Had the wind somehow teased it open? The wood hasp that held it shut was old; maybe the screws that held it in place had worked themselves loose.

The cypress-wood steps beneath Leenie's bare feet were as smooth as more than a hundred years of sun and wind and rain could make them. With the toes of her right foot she shoved the door all the way open. Its hinges complained softly. The inside of the cabin was dark as a cave. She fumbled in her pack for her flashlight; it was cool in her palm. She clicked it on.

In the dust directly across the threshold was a single footprint.

A sly finger of fear tickled the back of Leenie's neck. The footprint looked new; its edges had not yet been blurred by fresh dust. Why had that fool Lucy gone off to chase rabbits she could never catch? Leenie wondered uneasily. She directed the flashlight beam deeper into the darkness. There was another footprint. And another.

Sometimes you could be so scared about what might happen next that your heart hammered hard enough to rock your whole body, Leenie realized. She steadied herself and tried to regard the footprints calmly. They didn't travel in a straight line, she noticed. They were staggery, like they'd been made by a person who was sick or hurt or drunk, maybe.

Leenie let her flashlight beam follow the footprints all the way across the floor of the cabin.

Axel Erickson lay in the southwest corner of the room. His eyes were shut and it looked like he wasn't breathing. His shirt was torn at the collar and there was a gash on his forehead where blood had clotted in a thick ridge the color of tar.

“Axel?” Leenie called. The sound of his name on her lips sounded queer. It had no place on Sugar Island. Was he trying to fake her out for some reason? If she walked up to him right now, would he rise up suddenly, grab hold of her leg, and throw her down on the floor?

“You okay, Mr. Erickson?” she called louder. It sounded weird to call him “Mr.” because in lots of ways he didn't look much older than Chuckie. She stayed safely on the porch, ready to run like a rabbit if she had to. She could hear Lucy barking enthusiastically on the far side of the island. The branches of the magnolia tree brushed the tin roof; a cricket called from under the porch. But Axel Erickson didn't move and he didn't answer.

8

"Axel?" Maybe a third attempt to rouse him would be the charmed one, Leenie hoped. Still the photographer did not move.

Leenie grabbed her pack off the porch, followed his staggery footprints across the room, and knelt beside him. She laid the flashlight down; its beam slanted crazily against the cypress rafters overhead. Gingerly, she reached out to touch his shoulder. He'd looked so thin and wimpy that morning two weeks ago when she'd watched him row out to the middle of Hadley; now she was startled to find that the flesh under her fingers was stringy with muscle.

"It's me," she called softly. "It's Leenie O'Brien, from back there at the Dew Drop. You get hurt or something?"

She was almost glad he couldn't hear. Clever observation, O'Brien; would he really be lying here like a sack of wet laundry if he hadn't gotten hurt? Just the same, when he did begin to stir, she hastily removed her hand from his shoulder and rocked back on her bare heels, ready for escape. It wasn't as if he was a person like Chuckie Bedell, after all, who was someone she'd once considered touching. Axel Erickson was a stranger; he was almost old; he was thinking about marrying a girl named Jane.

As Leenie watched, half-prepared for some calamity, the photographer opened his eyes. He stared without comprehension at the rafters overhead. He blinked several times, like someone coming slowly to the surface of a dream, even made small paddling motions in the air with his hands. Finally, his dreamy gray gaze came to rest on her face.

What if he doesn't remember who I am? Leenie worried. That would make being alone with him on Sugar Island in the middle of the night a lot scarier than it already was.

"It's you . . ." he whispered faintly, "the little orphan . . . who said she didn't know anything about . . . the swamp."

If he remembers that stuff about orphans, Leenie realized, then he really remembers. "Who'd you expect," she quipped, annoyed with herself for having invented such an elaborate lie in the first place, "Scarlett O'Hara?"

Axel Erickson passed his hands over his face as if he were checking for missing parts. "Didn't I warn you about the swamp?" Leenie demanded. "But no, you had to come out here and find out for yourself. Now look what's happened. You practically got killed. I think you ought to have stuck to taking pictures of old men on park benches, if you want my opinion."

The photographer propped himself up on one elbow. "When it started to rain," he explained in a faint voice, "I didn't think it would amount to much. Then the wind came up and I knew I couldn't make it back to the inn. I tried to beach the boat on this island . . . only something hit me and the boat slipped away and I knew I had to get my camera gear to a safe place . . . it was kind of a mess. . . ."

"A mess is right," Leenie agreed smugly. So it *had* been a boat she'd seen, light green like all of Granda's boats, and the writing on it had been *No. 12*.

Axel Erickson sat up and leaned his forehead against his bent knees. "Whew! I feel like I'd just been run over by a train," he groaned.

Leenie rummaged around in her pack. "I've got some aspirin here," she offered. "Alcohol and Band-Aids, too. I'll clean up that cut on your head." She searched for a clean pair of socks and stuck them under the neck of the flashlight so its beam glared straight into the photographer's face. He shielded his eyes and waved the light away.

"Would you please turn that thing off?" he begged weakly. "This isn't an operating room and I'm not a patient."

"You are now," Leenie corrected. And you almost got what you deserved, she nearly added. Instead, she plucked a cotton ball out of her first-aid kit. That was one thing Granda had insisted on—that she had to take a first-aid course at the county health center before he'd let her go alone into the swamp.

"This won't hurt much," she assured Axel. She wetted the cotton with alcohol and scrubbed efficiently at his forehead. He flinched, then resigned himself to her attentions. "You have an unusual bedside manner," he complained wanly. "I bet you watch all the reruns of 'M.A.S.H.' after school, too."

He's being snide because he feels embarrassed, Leenie decided. She washed his forehead with alcohol until the black ridge of clotted blood had been cleaned away. She peered intently at the wound with the flashlight held close.

"It really isn't quite as bad as it looked," she informed him matter-of-factly. She peeled open a butterfly bandage and applied it so that the edges of the wound were pinched neatly together. "There. I guess you'll live," she announced.

"Thanks—I think," the photographer murmured. His voice was still thin, and he slumped away from her to rest against the wall of the cabin. He shut his eyes, and Leenie noticed that his upper lip was mustached with perspiration. She began to feel a twinge of sympathy. Maybe he used to worry about riding the subways in New York City, but to find himself without a boat on an island in the middle of a storm in a swamp must've been even scarier. She reached for her sleeping bag, took out the thin blanket inside it, and flattened the bag beside Axel.

"You better stretch out on this," she suggested. She half-expected him to argue; instead he rolled gratefully onto the pallet without a word of protest.

"Do you have something to sleep on? I feel like sort of a jerk taking your—"

"Forget it. I've got a blanket. I'll fold it in half; it'll be thick enough for who it's for."

She wondered if that might make him smile. It didn't. Instead, he lay on the sleeping bag like somebody who'd been in a war, bandaged and pale, with dark blue shadows under his closed eyes. Leenie pulled the tab off a can of raspberry soda. It fizzed over so she wiped the rim of the can on the edge of her shirt. She held the can out, along with two aspirin.

"Better take these," she advised. "Otherwise, you'll feel almost as bad tomorrow as you do right now." The photographer raised his head enough to pop the pills into his mouth and take two swigs of soda, then waved the can aside. Leenie wiped the lip of the can again and drank the rest of its contents herself. In a few moments, Axel Erickson was as still as he'd been when she first found him.

Leenie tiptoed to the opposite corner of the cabin and spread her blanket on the floor. She stuck her socks in a spare T-shirt to make herself a pillow, lay down, and shut off the flashlight. Lucy had finally given up rabbit-catching and thrashed wetly into the cabin to collapse happily at Leenie's side.

Leenie dug her fingers into Lucy's thick neck ruff and stared into the darkness overhead. I had so looked forward to being all alone out here, she mused, but here I am, stuck with company I never asked for.

"Hey, Orphan Annie, you still awake?" came a drowsy voice from across the room. Not only am I not alone, Leenie thought, my company is a guy who thinks he's some kind of comedian.

"So I'm awake," she answered.

"I just wanted to tell you the swamp seems a whole lot better now that somebody else is on this island with me."

Speak for yourself, she wanted to answer. The photographer's breathing grew steady and soft across the room. Lucy began to snore. Leenie closed her own eyes. What would Sooz say if she knew I was out here with a guy older than Buck? she wondered. Not that there would be anything particular to tell about the whole adventure. Hardly anything at all, in fact. After all, romance is not my specialty, Leenie remembered sleepily. She pulled Lucy closer and slept herself.

9

When Leenie woke, the tiny cabin was filled with velvety gray dawn. The air that spilled over the windowsill behind her (the glass had been broken out long ago) was fragrant with perfume from the blooms on the old magnolia tree beside the porch. Cobwebs softened the edges of the hand-hewn cypress rafters over her head. The familiar peach crate she'd nailed to the wall beside the door still held the tin plates, bent silverware, and plastic water jugs she'd hauled out to the island three years ago.

Home, Leenie thought with quiet delight; I'm back where I belong, where I can be me. Mary Alice had been wrong: a person could go home again. Leenie smiled to herself, stretched, and reached for Lucy's soft, pale ears. Her fingers closed on air.

Leenie sat up so quickly she made herself dizzy. The memory of the previous night careened through the open window like a night hawk searching for a safe place to roost.

But I'm not alone out here, she remembered. That guy from cabin twelve is here with me and last night I bandaged up his head and— But when she glanced at the sleeping bag on the other side of the room, she saw it was empty. Lucy was nowhere to be seen either. What if the photographer had kidnapped Lucy, stolen the *Swamp Rat,* just taken off?

Then Leenie heard the creak of the old well sweep in the yard. She crawled to the window on her hands and knees and rose to peer over the edge of the sill.

Axel Erickson was shakily filling a metal pail that Leenie had left hanging on a nail on the porch. She watched as he poured water over his head and shivered in the misty dawn. Lucy sat nearby, observing the goings-on with concern. The photographer grimaced as if in pain, squeezed water out of his thick, bronze hair, then tipped the pail to his lips.

"Hold it!" Leenie screeched with alarm. "Don't drink any of that stuff till I run it through a filter!" Wasn't it bad enough that he had a lump on his head the size of a turtle egg? What he didn't need right now was a good case of backpacker's fever to go along with it.

She jammed her bare feet into her tennies and grabbed the Kleen-Water filter out of her pack. It weighed less than two pounds, was about the size of a flashlight, and had a pore size of .2 microns, which was small enough to screen out giardia cysts. Better yet, a quart of drinkable water could be filtered through it in three minutes. Sure, drinking water could be purified by boiling it hard for fifteen minutes, but that meant gathering wood and building a roaring fire, which always took more time than she was willing to spend.

Scowling and wishing she'd taken time to comb her hair with her fingers, Leenie hustled outside and snatched the water pail from the photographer. She set the filter in the mouth of a plastic jug she'd plucked off the shelf of her peach crate cupboard and poured the water through it. She carefully avoided looking at her unwished-for companion. It was too early in the morning for anything so personal. Instead, she studied the air about a foot above his head.

''Sorry,'' he apologized. His voice still sounded rusty. ''I guess I didn't stop to wonder if the water out here was safe to drink,'' he admitted.

''Guess you didn't,'' Leenie agreed. ''You sure would've if you'd ever had a case of backpacker's fever, though,'' she informed him. ''Some people call it beaver fever; that's because beavers can carry the giardia cysts and spread the bug from creek to creek, swamp to swamp.'' She paused and added pointedly: ''Other folks call it General Lee's revenge.'' She filled a tin cup and held it out to him.

''Here's to Dixie.'' He smiled ruefully, and drank.

The bruise that surrounded the Band-Aid on the photographer's forehead, Leenie noticed, was the same shade as grape jam, and since he was still very pale his freckles seemed as large and dark as chocolate chips. ''Bet you've got a headache,'' she observed. There was no sense being nasty to him, she decided; after all, they'd have to put up with one another for a few more hours.

The photographer shrugged and poured himself a second drink of water. ''As you warned me last night, Orphan Annie, I'll probably live.'' He winked at her over the edge of the tin cup.

''Soon as you feel a little better, I'll haul you back to the Dew Drop,'' she told him. Not that she'd had any intention in the world of going back there so soon. After all, what kind of revenge would it be if she only stayed away for a few hours? Axel Erickson limped to the porch and lowered himself carefully onto the bottom step. He's still worried maybe he broke something, Leenie suspected. She watched him squint reflectively into the misty dawn.

''Thanks,'' he murmured. He didn't sound particularly grateful, she noticed.

What's his problem now? she wondered crossly. You rented a cabin, mister, she ought to tell him, you didn't rent the right to go noodling all over Sawmill Swamp like you did. She drew a second pail of water and poured half of it over her head. She dug the sleep out of her eyes, twisted her long dark hair into a single thick rope, wrung the water out of it. When she straightened herself, water trickled down her spine and soaked the waistband of her jeans.

"You don't sound exactly thrilled about going back," she groused. "But your rent's only paid until the end of the month," she pointed out, "which is only ten days away, so you'd have to be leaving pretty soon anyhow."

"Right—but without getting what I came down here after in the first place," he countered. "Namely, pictures of the swamp." He waved a hand to include the cypresses beyond Sugar Island, the smoky water, the air itself. He laced his fingers together and let his hands dangle between his knees. He shrugged. "So much for the best-laid plans, huh?"

"You didn't get *any* pictures of Sawmill?" Leenie asked.

"Nary a one. But of course you're absolutely right about going back to the inn. That fellow who's been looking after you, that Mr. O'Brien, will definitely not be thrilled when he finds out you're out here all alone with some photographer from New York." He paused suddenly, knitted his bronze brows together, and studied her more closely than she found comfortable.

"By the way—what *are* you doing out here? I thought you said you didn't know anything about the swamp."

Leenie let her glance slide carefully away from his and hoped she didn't look furtive. This whole business is getting pretty sticky, she realized. "Remember that social worker I told you about," she began slowly, "the one who was coming to get me?" The photographer nodded. "Well, she showed up all right," Leenie explained, "so I gave her the old slipperoo. Lucy and me headed straight for this place, which I know as well as I know my own hand."

Axel Erickson considered her confession for a moment. "Maybe that wasn't too smart, Leenie," he observed quietly. How come the sound of her name on his lips seemed different than it'd ever sounded before? Leenie wondered. "What I mean is, that social worker is going to think Mr. O'Brien can't keep track of you, that you just go wandering off to places like this any time you feel like it. She'll get the idea that you're kind of, well, wild."

"Look, there's wild and then there's *wild,*" Leenie objected. "I'm not wild the way some people use that word." Like they used it in regard to Mary Alice, for instance, which unfortunately was not something she could explain to someone like Axel Erickson. "Take for example my girl friend Sooz," Leenie went on. "She's going around now with a guy both of us have known since first grade. She says she got the urge to merge. I don't even want to think about the kind of trouble she could get into with an idea like that."

Axel smiled at her the same way a person might smile at a child, Leenie noticed. "Just the same," he murmured, "I don't want to be responsible for hurting *your* reputation."

"Nobody can say anything worse about me than's already been said," Leenie shot back. "Besides, Gran—Mr. O'Brien, I mean—knows where I'm at and he knows I'm as safe out here as if I was in church.'' She rubbed the inside of her arm. It was cool and wet. She hugged herself.

''You know what Mr. O'Brien told me once?'' she asked, shivering. ''He said if a person was careful, you could hear the echoes of dinosaurs out here. Did you know once dinosaurs lived in places just like Sawmill? Only when the swamps shrank up, and the water got low like it is now and food got scarce, then they were gone for good.''

''The echoes of dinosaurs,'' Axel Erickson repeated. His voice was soft with wonder. ''Hey, I like that! It has kind of a poetic ring. I think you've been pretty lucky to have had your Mr. O'Brien.'' The photographer's voice was deep and smooth and easy to listen to. Even so, it still made Leenie uncomfortable to look straight at him. Then she realized he wasn't looking at her, either.

''Listen, we better get our stuff together,'' he sighed. ''The sooner we get back to the inn, the less cause Mr. O'Brien will have to worry, right?''

Leenie cleared her throat. ''Not necessarily. Like I told you, he knows where I am. I left a note for him, said I'd be back in a few days. So if you still want 'em, I can help you get your pictures. What I'll do is, maybe I'll make you a deal.''

''A deal?'' Axel Erickson raised his eyebrows and looked vaguely alarmed.

''Sure. I'll give you a guided tour of the swamp if you'll show me how to take pictures.''

He seemed more astonished than ever. ''I had no idea you were interested in photography!''

''I wasn't until a few days ago,'' Leenie admitted. ''Remember I mentioned Sooz a minute ago? Well, she and Chuckie Bedell are hanging out all the time now. There's no room for me—and when school starts, it'll be even worse. They'll be close as spoons in a drawer. I figured I'd get on the school paper; that'd give me plenty to do—and it'd help a lot if I knew how to take pictures. I could cover the games, all that stuff. I'd be so busy I'd never know if they were making out or not."

No grateful look crossed Axel Erickson's face at the prospect of getting a guided tour through the swamp, however. "What's the matter?" Leenie heard herself demand angrily. "You changed your mind already? So forget I offered! Go ahead and take pictures of the Everglades. So what if they've already been photographed a million times and Sawmill's never been photographed once!"

"Simmer down, Leenie," he cautioned. Once again, her name sounded soft and easy on his lips. "You still haven't convinced me that Mr. O'Brien is going to understand any of this, not to mention that social worker you told me about. She could cause you a lot of grief. Ever stop to think about that?"

She's already caused me plenty of grief, Leenie wanted to snap back. A tardy realization dawned on her: a fib could take on a life of its own. It demanded care and maintenance. You had to keep nudging it down the road in front of you, otherwise it sneaked up behind you like a junkyard dog.

"That social worker—well, she isn't exactly a social worker," Leenie began. "She's Mr. O'Brien's daughter actually not a social worker at all that was a lie I told you and her name is Mary Alice but she's never been married only she went away to live in Boston sixteen years ago after she had a baby out of wedlock which was me." It was ungrammatical and didn't have any punctuation, Leenie realized, but the main thing was to get to the end of the confession before she decided not to make it.

There was no way now for her to avoid his glance. Leenie found herself staring straight into the photographer's gravel-colored eyes. He stared levelly back at her. "Let me run that by again, just to see if I got it right," he murmured. "Mr. O'Brien had a daughter named Mary Alice . . . she had a baby sixteen years ago but she wasn't married . . . so Mr. O'Brien is actually your grandfather and you're—"

"Illegitimate," Leenie confirmed. "No apologies, okay? I mean, I didn't have anything to do with it. None of it was my fault. I don't even know who my father was. All it says on my birth certificate is 'Father Unknown.' But I don't care who he is; Mary Alice doesn't matter, either. They dumped me when I was three months old and now it's my turn to dump them."

"Vengeance is mine, sayeth Leenie O'Brien," Axel Erickson mused. He tapped one front tooth with an index finger and studied her closely. "But you didn't have to tell me any of this," he pointed out.

Leenie inspected her fingernails, which, she noticed with faint surprise, were quite dirty. "I wanted to," she admitted. "You told me about Jane and how you guys were going to write books together—and I wanted you to know about me, that's all."

But was that all? Leenie wondered. Something more fundamental was involved, she realized, but when she searched her heart for it, it eluded her like a bluegill slipping off into the dark shadow of a bank of maiden cane.

"What I feel like is . . . is something that happened by accident," she explained. Until this instant, she'd never been able to quite put it into words, but something in Axel Erickson's patient gray eyes made it suddenly easier. She flattened her dark, wet bangs against her forehead and went on.

"See, none of them ever planned on me—not Mary Alice or my father and for sure not my grandparents. I suppose that's why my Gramma never really liked me—I was just too much of a surprise. Only now Mary Alice has come back and she wants to forget about the past—except that's what I am—I'm yesterday's daughter. If she forgets the past, she better forget about me, too."

It seemed to Leenie that Axel Erickson was looking at her as if he'd never seen her before. "Yesterday's daughter," he echoed softly, as if the two words had some kind of magic in them. "Well, if yesterday's daughter will show me Sawmill Swamp, it'd be my pleasure to show her how to take pictures. Do we have a deal?" He held out his hand.

"We have a deal," Leenie answered, and in the cool gray dawn that was slowly brightening over Sugar Island, they carefully shook hands.

10

"So where do you want to start?" Leenie asked as they rinsed their breakfast plates clean of tuna fish and cracker crumbs. She started another quart of drinking water through the Kleen-Water filter into the plastic jug. "There're dozens of places we could go," she told Axel. "I guess mostly it depends on what kinds of pictures you want to get."

A purple dragonfly stitched its way through the misty air and landed in the magnolia tree. The photographer smiled and when he did, Leenie noticed crinkles appeared at the corners of his gray eyes. Now that she'd quit lying to him, it was easier to look right at him.

"Before we leave the island, I'll for sure want to get shots of all this," he said, and waved a hand to include the cabin, the well sweep, the magnolia tree, "but to begin with, maybe you'd just like to show me some of your favorite places."

Leenie nodded. When he smiled like that it was hard not to smile right back at him. She permitted herself a grin, and a quirky feeling filtered into her heart like water was filtering into the jug at her feet. "Okay—let's start with the prairie."

"Prairie?" Axel Erickson snorted. "You mean I'm really in North Dakota? I always thought a prairie was a chunk of flat land out west that was covered with grass and flowers."

"It is," Leenie assured him, "but down here we add plenty of water. Our prairies are covered with grass and flowers, too, but they grow out of a couple of feet of water instead of out of the ground. C'mon; I'll show you."

Together they loaded the *Swamp Rat* with raspberry soda, a gallon jug of filtered water, crackers, two towels, and all of Axel's camera gear. After Lucy piled into the boat, Leenie laid her fishing pole beside the punt pole.

"Are we going fishing, too?" Axel wanted to know.

"Not we, me," Leenie corrected. "While you're snapping away, I'll try to catch us something to eat for supper."

But as Axel stepped into the *Swamp Rat,* he stumbled and almost dove in head first. He sat down, shaky and pale, on the nearest bench, the color drained from his face.

"You don't look too hot," Leenie observed. "Maybe we ought to stay right here. You could go back to the cabin and forget about taking any pictures."

Axel dismissed her suggestion with an impatient wave of his hand. "It's important to get these pictures and then get back to the inn," he reminded her. "And I sure hope you're right, little lady, when you say your grandfather will understand the two of us traipsing around out here—not to mention your mother."

"Trust me, Granda will understand," Leenie assured him. He would, too; otherwise, he'd never have let her go alone into the swamp when she was only twelve years old. As for Mary Alice, well, she wasn't entitled to have an opinion one way or the other. She'd given up that right a long time ago. Leenie almost told Axel so, then remembered his quip about *Vengeance is mine, sayeth Leenie O'Brien.* Better leave the subject of Mary Alice strictly alone, she decided.

Leenie pushed the *Swamp Rat* out of the soft muck at the edge of Sugar Island and poled the boat smoothly southward toward a tangle of fetterbush and inkberry and holly. In the near distance was a string of tiny islands, none of them more than a few feet square, where stands of young slash pine had taken hold. Beyond them, she knew, lay Ghost Prairie.

Half an hour later, the prairie spread before them, two feet of water that covered more than five acres of land but that nevertheless looked as solid as any western prairie. It was bordered on three sides by tall, golden maiden cane grass, against which an occasional clump of purple iris bloomed. Across the main expanse of the prairie bloomed other flowers—waxy white water lilies with golden centers, tall-stemmed bog buttons that looked like old-fashioned ladies' hat pins, and clusters of pale pink gerardias and meadow beauties, which all grew directly out of the water.

"The reason Granda calls this Ghost Prairie," Leenie explained, "is because lots of people have tried to hide in the swamp but some of 'em never made it back out again. Some of those folks, he says, are probably sleeping in the ooze right along with the dinosaurs. We might be floating over their bones right this minute."

Axel shuddered. "If it's okay with you, I'll just forget about bones and concentrate on these flowers. If you can keep the boat from rocking too much, I'll try to get some long-range shots of the prairie. Later maybe we can figure out a way to set up the tripod so I can get some close-ups."

Leenie rested her punt pole across her knees and watched as the photographer loaded his camera, removed its neck strap, selected a lens from the many that lay each in its own compartment in the folded-out black camera case. He rested the body of the camera against his cheek and pressed his right eye to the eyepiece. With his left arm tucked against his ribs to steady himself, he began to take a series of long-range shots.

So this is what he'd been doing that day he took pictures of me in the lifeguard's tower, Leenie realized. It hadn't been anything personal at all; he'd never intended to invade her privacy or make some kind of fool out of her.

Leenie studied the back of the photographer's head and smoothed Lucy's ears to keep the dog from rocking the boat. The heavy mist had nearly dissipated so Axel's hair had become less curly; now, loose cinnamon-colored tendrils curled behind his ears. His T-shirt was cotton mesh and through it Leenie could see the epaulets of freckles on his shoulders.

She squinted into the distance. He was completely oblivious to her presence, so how come just to be here with him made her feel warm, even a little bit happy? It must be the sun, Leenie decided. Yes, it was the sun on Ghost Prairie that made her feel so good; it was just being back in the swamp that made her feel so contented. Only that; it wasn't anything more complicated. She bent her head and kissed Lucy between her blonde ears.

Click.

Leenie looked up, startled, to discover that the girl-kisses-dog scene had just been caught on film. "Not fair!" she fumed, not exactly displeased. "I should've straightened my hair! I bet I look like a wreck!" Was she really saying such dumb things?

"Forget about your hair. If I'd wanted a beautiful model, I'd have stayed in New York, which has got 'em wall to wall."

"Thanks. You just made my day."

Axel's laugh was an amused little bark that made Lucy cock her ears and thump her tail against the floor of the boat. "I didn't mean that exactly the way it came out," he apologized. "What I meant to say, Leenie, is that you're different."

Once again, the sound of her name on his lips had such a soft, sweet ring. "Different how?" she wanted to know. Did he think she looked like Huckleberry Finn, too? While he reloaded his camera, she rose, faced him, and began to stroke the *Swamp Rat* deeper into Ghost Prairie.

"It's like I told you back there at the inn," Axel explained. "You have a leggy, natural grace that is quite charming." He trained the camera on her. "You're strong and beautiful the same way a yearling racehorse is." *Click.* "But I think you've been a tomboy for so long that"—*Click*—"you don't really know what you look like." *Click.* He'd managed to catch her in each phase of poling—pressing the pole against the peaty floor of the swamp, leaning hard against it, raising it up, starting all over again.

Leenie paused, hooked her right arm around the punt pole and cradled it under her armpit. "I suppose I'm a tomboy because—" The reason seemed close, she could almost catch hold of it, yet the moment she reached for it, it slid away from her like a bar of soap on a shower floor.

"Because it's easier?" Axel finished for her.

The instant he put it into words, Leenie knew it was the truth. Yes; it had been easier. Easier not to be a girl, easier to ignore the fact you'd awakened one morning in a body that didn't belong to you. But there was more to it than that.

"If I'm a tomboy," she tried to explain, "then for sure I won't ever have to worry about ending up like Mary Alice."

"Ending up like Mary Alice? Is she really that bad? I mean, what I'm getting here is a mental picture of snaggly yellow teeth, hair like moldy rope, and dog breath. Like she's a real witch."

Overhead the sun was like a brass shield in the sky. Leenie shaded her eyes against its glare. In person, Mary Alice had been exactly like her high school picture, plain, pretty, a person who neither smiled nor frowned. Nothing like a witch. Just the same, she couldn't get off scot-free.

"Hey, did your mom dump *you?*" Leenie countered. "Bet she didn't. My friends' mothers didn't dump them, either. But old Mary Alice unloaded me like my name was Harold."

"Harold? I thought you said you didn't know what your dad's name was," Axel murmured, surprised.

"Harold is a rabbit," Leenie explained with exaggerated patience. "He's white, wears a red leather collar, and right now he's locked up at the county animal shelter because somebody got rid of him just like Mary Alice got rid of me."

"Poor Harold. But back to Mary Alice—why don't you talk to her about all this? Maybe there were good reasons why she—"

"Reasons, schmeasons," Leenie interrupted. "But if it's reasons you want to talk about, the reason I'm out here right now is because I don't want to discuss *any*thing with her. She never gave me a chance sixteen years ago and now I won't give her one, not till the twelfth of never."

"What happens on the twelfth of never?"

"Nothing. The twelfth of never never comes, that's the whole point. If it's all the same to you, let's drop the subject. You said you wanted to set up a tripod—so how about if we tie up on that itty bitty island over there?" She pointed briskly to one of the new islands with its half-dozen rootlings of slash pine.

Once on the island, Leenie was relieved to see that Axel set aside the subject of Mary Alice. He situated his tripod on the narrow strip of beach, mounted his camera on it, and began to take close-up shots of rose pogonias, pale-green pitcher plants, and yellow colic root.

Leenie walked to the opposite side of the island, scarcely twelve feet away, and within thirty minutes managed to catch a nice string of bluegills. She cleaned them, then lathered her hands with leaves from a soap bush—Granda said it was actually a Virginia willow—and carefully cleaned her fingernails with a tiny stick from the beach. When she returned to Axel's side of the island, he beckoned her over to the camera.

"Your turn now. There are three frames left on this roll and they've got your name on 'em." Leenie bent to peer through the viewfinder. "Now adjust your focusing ring," Axel directed, "and bring your subject into view."

After a minute of fiddling with the focusing ring, Leenie got a water lily in view. "You might have a depth-of-field problem to solve," Axel warned. "In other words, do you want everything in the frame evenly focused, do you want to bring your main subject into sharp focus, or do you want to let your background come forward? You're the artist; you decide."

As Leenie was about to snap the shutter, a bee lighted in the yellow heart of the lily. She focused on it until each hair of its body was acutely in focus. Then the bee rose unexpectedly out of the heart of the flower, trailing golden grains of pollen from its feet as it departed. Leenie snapped the shutter.

She turned to Axel, breathless. "Did you see that?" she marveled. "Pollen was dripping off that bee's feet like yellow sand!"

When Axel smiled, Leenie noticed his freckles squished into a single dark smudge across his nose. "I guess those kinds of accidents are the reason I love photography," he admitted. "It's as if you can look at life differently through a camera lens; things you wouldn't pay any mind to at other times become suddenly quite marvelous." He winked. "Maybe we'll have to renegotiate our deal—I might have to buy some of your pictures back and use 'em in the book, huh?"

"I'm not going to get that good in just a couple days," Leenie warned. When he grinned again, she heard herself demand abruptly, "How old are you, anyway?" All of a sudden, it was critically important to know.

He winked slyly. "Old enough to be your brother," he answered.

"That could mean anything," Leenie objected, "eighteen or twenty or—"

"Old enough to be your *big* brother," he amended, then added: "I'm twenty-four, if you must know. Jane's twenty-three."

You could've gone all day without telling me how old Jane is, Leenie nearly blurted. Actually, if he never mentioned her again, it would be even better. So he was twenty-four; that meant he was only eight years older than she was herself. Not such a big difference; after all, when he was thirty, she'd be twenty-two, nearly as grown-up as he was, right?

"And I'm old enough to know when it's quitting time," Axel announced. "Noontime is the pits for picture taking—the ambient light has a flat, hard quality about it because, with the sun straight overhead, there aren't any shadows to lend a photograph texture and contrast. So what d'you say we settle down right here, maybe eat some lunch, just loaf around until three, four o'clock?"

"Okay by me," Leenie agreed. When he bent his head to dismantle the camera and tripod, she noticed a star-shaped cowlick in the crown of his bronze hair. She was tempted to reach out to touch it. Was it as smooth as it looked? Instead, she popped the tops off two cans of raspberry soda and handed him one. She raised hers in a mock toast.

"Here's to lots of good pictures," she murmured. She was glad she'd cleaned her nails and that he hadn't said he was thirty-four. That would be too much of a difference. As it was, well, he wasn't all that much older than Buck. Not so much that she couldn't like him a little. Right? Right, Leenie decided.

11

At four o'clock, Axel began to shoot again. He got more pictures of Ghost Prairie with a western light on it, which, he told Leenie, was a lot different than eastern light, although to her it looked almost the same. Then he got at least a dozen shots of a flock of red-headed, yellow-legged gallinules as they raced across the tops of some lily pads searching for bugs to feed on. Later, when several white ibises returned to their rookery in the tops of a few dead cypresses at the edge of the prairie, they too were captured on film. The end of the roll was taken up with portraits of three thumb-sized squirrel frogs and a pair of box turtles with vividly spotted shells.

By six-thirty, it seemed to Leenie that he'd taken pictures of almost everything that deserved to be photographed. There was one place left to take him, however. She hadn't mentioned it to him before because she hadn't made up her mind whether to show it to him at all.

"You want to go inside a cypress bay?" she asked, surprised to discover she'd made up her mind. "It's what most folks think of when they think of swamps—you know, a dim, dark, mysterious place that maybe looks like the world did when it first started."

"You've got my attention," Axel declared, "only what, exactly, is a bay?"

"Just a place where cypresses grow real thick," Leenie told him. "Because their foliage is so heavy, the sun hardly ever shines inside a bay. The water looks black all the time, never blue, and the moss hangs down from the tree branches like gray curtains, like in a spook movie." She poled slowly toward the spiky row of cypress tops in the distance. "Mostly, I go visit the bay when I want to get my head straight. In there, it's easy to close the world out. Nothing matters except you, the trees, the water."

Leenie realized Axel was studying her attentively, and she felt a rush of embarrassment. He probably thought she was a little loony; first she'd talked about dinosaurs and old bones, now she was into closing out the world. Blabbermouth O'Brien, she thought uneasily.

But when Axel spoke, his voice was gentle and understanding. "You love this whole place, don't you, Leenie?" Whenever he spoke her name like that, her heart softened toward him as well as toward a person named Leenie O'Brien.

"It's the truth, I do," she admitted. "Out here, it's as if I know who I am." He had winked at her lots of times, so now Leenie tried one on him. "Maybe I'm not exactly a tomboy, but I *am* a swamp rat!" She hesitated, then confided what else she'd been thinking, especially since Sooz and Chuckie got to be such an item. "What I'd like to be someday is a person who studies places like Sawmill, like forest rangers study forests, you know? You think that's a dumb idea?"

"Hardly. You'd be good at it because you liked it, Leenie."

At the edge of the bay, Leenie cleared a path through a tangle of holly with the tip of her punt pole, then the boat slid easily into the somber, dark waters of the bay. Inside, there was no incessant chatter of birds, no trilling of frogs. Instead there was the steady, hypnotic drip of moisture from the branches of the cypress, the eerie noiseless movement overhead of sheer gray-green curtains of Spanish moss.

"That stuff isn't Spanish and it isn't moss," Leenie whispered. Something about the bay made you lower your voice, like when you went into a church. "Granda says it's an epiphyte, a rootless plant. It gets all the nourishment it needs from the air and rain, so it never damages the tree it's growing on. If you came back here in the springtime, you'd see it was covered all over with tiny yellow flowers that smell real sweet."

"You're the one who's sweet, Leenie, a real sweetheart for showing me a place like this!" Axel murmured, his voice as hushed as her own. He took up his camera and while he snapped away, Leenie listened to the breathing of the swamp, to the faint murmur of the water around the fluted black bases of the cypresses, to the ghostly swish of the filmy curtains draped from the tree branches. Even though it'd been warm all day, handkerchiefs of mist rose off the dark water and floated eerily away among the black tree trunks. *You're sweet,* he'd said, *a real sweetheart.*

Axel passed the camera to Leenie. "Here, you take a few frames," he suggested. Leenie had sat in the bay dozens of times, but this time, through the viewfinder, a row of familiar cypresses backlighted by the sinking sun looked like monks at vespers. Leenie framed them carefully and snapped. When she switched from a horizontal to a vertical format, an owl swooped across the viewfinder, silent and silver-winged; she snapped again.

When the roll of film was finished, they sat wordlessly, not eager to leave or to speak. The boat listed quietly in the water; a few rags of mist drifted past; from deeper in the bay came the throaty call of the owl who'd been disturbed. Axel turned slowly. "Thanks, Leenie," he whispered. "I owe you one."

Leenie swallowed hard and eased the *Swamp Rat* out of the bay. To the west the black branches of a grove of mature slash pine clung futilely onto the dying sun, but it slipped below the horizon's dark edge, leaving only a scarlet stain in the sky. As they poled toward Sugar Island, the water around the punt turned mauve, then faded to silver. In the east, a three-quarter yellow moon rested like an enormous chick in the abandoned nest of an egret.

"What a perfect way to end a perfect day," Axel sighed, and turned to face the island. Leenie studied the back of his head, the bronze hair curling behind his ears, the square set of his lean shoulders. But I don't want it ever to end, she realized. It's been the nicest day in my whole life and I want it to go on forever.

Smoke curled up from the campfire as pale as breath. Overhead, the moon was now as white as a dinner plate in the indigo sky. The Big Dipper—Granda said in England it was called The Plough—was tipped so the water could run out. Leenie laid each bluegill on its own piece of tinfoil, sprinkled each with salt, stuck a lemon wedge in the body cavity of each, sealed the tinfoil, and laid the envelopes on the hot stones at the edge of the fire.

Later, when they'd licked their fingers clean and polished off the last two cans of raspberry soda, Axel decided he'd been wrong.

"*This* was the best way to end the day," he declared, "with a nice fire, a great fish supper—and a charming dinner companion!"

They rinsed their plates, then sat cross-legged on opposite sides of the fire. There are so many things I want to say, Leenie thought, only I don't even know how to start. "Penny for your thoughts," Axel teased after a long silence.

Leenie picked at a hole in the knee of her jeans and was glad that, in the firelight, he would not be able to see that her cheeks were flushed. "I want to thank you, too," she mumbled.

"For showing you a few basics about picture-taking? Forget it. Like I said, I owe you one. You rescued me from a fate worse than death—or whatever might've happened to me if you hadn't come along when you did."

"I just want you to know it's been nice to know you, you know?" Leenie persisted. How many times had she just said *know?* She plunged ahead without counting. "After today, see, I'll always look at the swamp and Sugar Island differently. Just because you've been here. So, well, anyway, thanks a lot."

"What're friends for?" Axel teased lightly, and unfolded himself from his place on the other side of the fire. "But right now, little chum, I think we better get ourselves some shut-eye. We ought to be up early and headed back to the inn before the sun's up, right?"

"Right," Leenie agreed without enthusiasm. Reluctantly, she banked earth around the campfire, then poured water over it. It sizzled fiercely; then the only light on the island came from the moon above. She turned and hurried toward the cabin. In a few days he'd go back to his other life. She'd go back to being Leenie O'Brien. It would all be over.

There was one more thing she wanted to tell him. She turned suddenly just after she mounted the bottom step of the porch. Axel had followed so close behind her that she found herself staring straight into his eyes. In the silver light his irises were no longer gray but black; his bronze hair was a dark helmet over his head.

She forgot what she'd planned to say. She only had to lean forward an inch or two to kiss him on the lips. She did, lightly.

Afterward, Leenie couldn't remember exactly how her arms got around his neck. That part must've been easy, too. His mouth tasted earthily of sunshine, salt, and fish. She kissed him again, not so lightly this time. At first, he didn't kiss her back. When he did, he circled her ribs with his arms, pulled her so close she could feel the length of his thin body against her own, and kissed her long and slowly.

"Oh, Leenie," he groaned when he stepped back, "wild and lovely Leenie!" There was an ache in his voice that made Leenie reach for him again. "Leenie, Leenie, don't," he begged. "We can't do this."

"Why not?" she heard herself say. There was an ache in her own voice. "This has been the most perfect day in my whole life and I don't ever want it to end!"

Axel carefully took her arms from around his neck. He folded her hands in his own, gently kissed the inside of each wrist, then held her at arm's length.

"Leenie, you're older than you think you are," he reminded her.

"I know I am," she choked. "Old enough to love you, that's how old!" Was that what she'd intended to say?

"Then you know the hardest part of loving can be letting go," he murmured softly. He kissed the tip of her nose the same way a brother might have, released her wrists, and hurried past her into the darkness of the cabin.

Leenie stared, unblinking, at the moon. It had all been so sweet, so easy! His lips had tasted so good, his body against her own had felt so dear, so *right*. For a few moments it seemed like the most important thing in the world was just to hang onto him, not to think about anything else.

Did that young dude from New York come on to you? Hazel had asked suspiciously. But that isn't what happened at all, Leenie realized. It was *me*. I was the one who came on to him. I wanted to hold him, hug him, kiss him until neither one of us could breathe.

She sat down on the bottom step of the porch and leaned weakly against the newel post. Is this what'd happened to Mary Alice sixteen years ago? she wondered numbly. Had it been as sweet and easy for her to do what I almost did, might've done, too, if Axel hadn't had more brains than me? It was a funny thing about the twelfth of never: it was a point in time that was never supposed to arrive. But Leenie suspected it just had.

12

It was five A.M. when Leenie docked the *Swamp Rat* in front of the Dew Drop Inn. The beach was deserted; all the Little Cabins were dark and quiet. Lucy plunged overboard, as glad to be home as she'd been to leave two days earlier. Leenie reached for her gear while Axel shouldered his camera bag and picked up his tripod.

"Listen to me a minute, Leenie. I think I know exactly how you feel," he began.

"*You* listen to *me*—you don't!" she countered coolly. "You're a photographer, not a mind-reader. Even if you were a mind-reader, there's no way in the world you could know what's in mine!"

"Let me finish, Leenie." He studied her earnestly, which was even more annoying. "It's okay by me if your feelings are hurt—maybe mine would be too if I were in your shoes—but it's not okay if you believe I betrayed you somehow. It would've been so easy out there to—well, you know what I mean." He tried to brush her chin gently with his knuckles but Leenie ducked her head and jerked away. Sure, she thought bitterly, now it's the old just-one-of-the-guys routine. One minute he calls me lovely Leenie (it still hurt to remember how sweet the words had sounded!), the next minute he treats me like a jock.

"If you stay mad, Leenie, it'll be hard to finish our work," he reminded her evenly.

"What work?" she blazed. "Didn't I get you back here all in one piece? I don't think I owe you much else!"

"I'm going to develop all our film this morning, Leenie. Why don't you stop by the cabin this afternoon and see how your frames turned out?" He was determined to be patient and understanding.

Leenie lifted one shoulder carelessly. She wanted to look at him, see herself reflected in his quiet gray eyes. "Maybe I will, maybe I won't," she muttered, and kept her glance averted. Was it possible, she wondered, to care about someone a lot (to even think you loved him, in fact) but to feel like you almost hated him, too? She resisted the temptation to brush his hand with her own, turned on her heel, and left him standing on the beach alone.

She skirted the side of the Big Cabin and went around to the back door. Agnes Abercrombie's replacement wasn't parked in the driveway, which meant Hazel hadn't arrived early. Good. The shades over Granda's bedroom windows were drawn; no doubt he was still sound asleep. Mary Alice would've had to sleep in the living room on the couch that pulled out into a bed. But the living room drapes were wide open; maybe that meant she'd come to her senses and gone back to Boston where she belonged.

What I'll do, Leenie decided, is tiptoe in, warm myself a quick cup of coffee, providing Granda forgot to empty the pot last night after supper, then I'll dive into bed and get a couple hours' decent sleep. Last night, she hadn't gotten a wink, had just lain there in her corner of the cabin, watched the shifting patterns of moonlight on the wall, had plenty of time to marvel about what a fool she'd almost been.

Leenie eased herself through the kitchen door. The coffee smelled awfully fresh. Darn! In the early-morning gloom of the kitchen, Mary Alice sat at the table with her hands folded around a steaming cup.

"Good morning, Arl—Leenie, I mean," she said in the hushed tone of voice one uses when other people in the house are still asleep. She gestured with her coffee cup. "Would you like some, too?" Leenie nodded numbly.

"Daddy never liked me to drink coffee when I was your age," Mary Alice confided. "But he didn't always remember to pour it out, so sometimes I'd sneak a cup early in the morning." She smiled but Leenie refused to smile back. I won't tell her I've done the same thing, she decided; it'd only make her think we have something in common, and except for what almost happened out there on Sugar Island, we aren't anything alike.

"I figured for sure you'd be gone by now," she muttered instead.

"I couldn't have left until I knew what'd happened to you, Leenie. Especially after we realized that fellow from New York who rented cabin twelve was gone, too."

"How'd you find that out?"

"Hazel checked."

Good old Hazel. She better quit reading those dumb novels from Walser's. "What bugged you the most," Leenie demanded coolly, "knowing I was out in a bad storm or knowing I might be with some guy?"

Mary Alice hesitated. "Both, to be honest."

"No reason for you to get in a suds over any of this," Leenie informed her. "I got to be sixteen without much advice from you. I'd say it's a little late for you to do the concerned mother routine."

"Maybe we ought to talk about that, Leenie. The kind of mother I've been, not to mention other loose ends we should try to tie up."

Leenie feigned amusement. "Is that what you call my father?" she inquired with a sweet smile, "a loose end?" She was pleased to note that Mary Alice flushed deeply. "That's not exactly how *I* think of him," she confessed. "To me, he's Father Unknown, which, apparently, is how he wanted to be identified on my birth certificate." Leenie had never imagined being cruel could be such a pleasure. Was this how Sooz felt back in third grade when she laid on that news about being illegitimate?

Mary Alice massaged her temples with the tips of her fingers. "His name is Allen Lavarty, Leenie, and he's part of the reason I'm back in Wayburn right now. After all, I'm not the only parent you have."

"You going to give me a biology lesson?" Leenie murmured. "Don't bother—I already know how babies get here. We got that way back in fifth grade." She noticed that Mary Alice was awfully white. Even without makeup, though, she was pretty in a plain, quiet way. Stubborn, too, because she wouldn't let the conversation die a natural death.

"I know there're lots of things I can never make up to you," Mary Alice went on, "and I can't undo the past sixteen years. We can't ever be mother and daughter the way some mothers and daughters are, but I hoped we could learn to be—" Her voice got a crack in it and she had a hard time finishing what she wanted to say. "I hoped we could be friends, Leenie," she finally managed.

Leenie stared and felt the smile slide off her own face. "Friends?" she echoed. Did Mary Alice think the past could be cancelled out so easily, that she could offer a thin slice of friendship in place of what

Sooz had had with her mom? "I suppose you want me to be friends with *him*, too," Leenie said. At least Mary Alice's name had been on that piece of paper; he hadn't even offered that much.

"He's willing if you are, Leenie." Suddenly, Mary Alice remembered the coffee. She got a second cup and filled it. "Cream or sugar?" she asked, and snugged her bathrobe around herself.

"Cream," Leenie said automatically. "But how do you know what he wants?"

"We've been talking about it, Leenie. About what we did sixteen years ago. We both think we owe you a chance to know who your parents were. Are, I mean."

Leenie picked up her cup and rose from the table. "It's too late," she said stonily. "I'm just something that happened to you guys. Now you want to treat me like a project, something that'll make you feel better about yourselves. Well, I'm Leenie O'Brien, an illegitimate swamp rat. There's nothing you can do that'll ever change that." She walked down the hall to her room and shut the door behind her.

When she sat down on the edge of her bed, however, she had to look at the pictures taped to the back of the door. The eyes of the girl in the picture were dark and brooding. Her legs were long and strong and brown. *Wild and wonderful Leenie,* Axel Erickson had whispered with an aching voice. Had he loved her a little, just a little?

Leenie peeled off her jeans and crawled into bed. She pulled the sheet over her head to make a tent. Her whole life had turned into such a mess: she had parents she didn't want, loved a person who was too old for her, and, worst of all, last night the twelfth of never had arrived.

* * *

It'd been pretty simple to give Mary Alice a hard time. Hazel Grobey, however, was a fish from another pond. "Your Granda ought to take a paddle to your fanny!" she fumed. "Leaving that snippy note for him at the lifeguard's tower like you did—not even starting it out with 'Dear Granda'! If you'd been mine, sweet pea, I'd have jumped into a boat, gone straight out there to that island, would've hauled you right back here by that long, black hair of yours!"

Hazel smoothed her bangs away from her forehead, and Leenie pressed them deliberately back in place again. "Well, I'm not and you didn't," she mumbled, then took a moment to study Hazel critically. She looked suspiciously thinner and was wearing a pair of pink tennies that didn't have holes in their sides. "You on a diet or something?" Leenie demanded.

"Don't change the subject," Hazel warned. "We are not discussing the fact I started counting calories two weeks ago, we are talking about your antics. That man—or boy or whatever he is who rented cabin twelve—was gone from here the same time you were. Am I to assume the two of you were together out there in the middle of that swamp?"

"You are to assume we met purely by accident," Leenie groaned. "It was no big romantic plot. I've already told you at least once that he's going to marry someone named Jane. As for me, I'm going to—"

"Make nervous wrecks out of the whole family," Hazel lamented. Her warm butterscotch eyes were pained. Leenie inclined her head toward her collarbone. How come Hazel was talking about the family like she was really part of it? Leenie wondered. Maybe she'd been Ass't. Mgr. at the Dew Drop so long she thought she was.

"I gotta go check on my photographs," Leenie announced, since Hazel didn't seem to be able to wiggle off the hook by herself.

"*Your* photographs? Since when did you have any interest in—"

"Since yesterday," Leenie answered smoothly, and tried to squeeze her bones past Hazel's newly diminished ones. Hazel, however, trapped her in a pair of sunbrowned arms that once had hung Jeff Grobey out to dry.

"Listen, sweet cakes, we all love you, don't you know that?" she whispered. "Nobody wants to see you so mean and mad, not even Mary Alice. Especially Mary Alice. She came back here because she wants to try to make things right—"

"It's too late for right," Leenie insisted, and patiently removed Hazel's arms from her shoulders. She turned, slipped through the screen door, and headed for cabin twelve.

In Axel's cabin, wet photographs were strung on three plastic clotheslines that spanned the kitchen. Photos that were already dry were stacked in piles on the top of the snack bar. "Which ones are mine?" Leenie wanted to know right away. If they kept busy talking about pictures, they wouldn't have to talk about anything else. She'd debated about coming to the cabin at all. If she didn't, she'd finally decided, it would be like not reading the last chapter of one of Hazel's books, where the whole story was stitched together and the loose ends tied up. She wished, though, that she hadn't reminded herself about loose ends.

"That pile there is yours," Axel said and pointed to a stack on the end of the snack bar. "Four or five of 'em turned out real nice."

"Only four or five?"

"Don't feel bad! Sometimes a good photographer can shoot a couple hundred frames just to get a half dozen that're special."

Leenie had been sure she knew exactly what Sawmill Swamp and Sugar Island looked like, but the images that greeted her were somehow much different. The cypress-wood cabin was gilded with silver, the mist had softened the edges of the magnolia blooms so that the scene looked like something from a forgotten dream . . . the cypress bay was like the interior of a cathedral, somber but beautiful . . . the trees along the aisles of black water in the bay were stoic, robed monks.

"What you're seeing is just another side of what's been there all the time," Axel explained. "See, all of us take certain things for granted—even the things we love or hate—till after a while we don't really see them anymore. That's the photographer's job—at least I think it is—to make the ordinary extraordinary and vice versa."

Leenie turned to study Axel's pictures. She saw herself, poling the *Swamp Rat,* strong-legged and brown, smiling into the camera, no longer a crazy, brooding girl. "Do I really look like this?" she wondered out loud. The pictures on the back of her bedroom door showed someone quite different.

"That's one of you," Axel admitted. "Thing is, maybe there's more than one Leenie O'Brien."

Was there more than one Mary Alice, too? Leenie wondered. And a different Father Unknown than the one she was so sure she never wanted to know?

"Mary Alice has got this idea I should meet my father," Leenie blurted out. After what'd happened on the island, she'd never intended to speak to him about anything personal. Once again, she found it hard to look at him, too. She aimed her gaze through the archway into the living room where the picture of Jane still sat on the coffee table. "Mary Alice says she knows they can't be ordinary parents to me, but I guess they want to be friends."

Axel shuffled a pile of prints and began to sort them into smaller piles according to topic, trees in one pile, prairie shots in a different one, views of the cypress bay in yet another. "Sounds good to me, kid. After all, how can you ever know where you're headed if you don't know where you came from?"

"What kind of a dumb question is that?"

"They're where you came from, Leenie. You didn't hatch from an egg in some egret's nest out there in the swamp. Maybe you're lucky—some kids in your predicament never know who their parents are at all. You've got a chance to find out." He slipped the smaller piles of photos into large plastic envelopes. "Which is not to say you gotta like 'em, much less love 'em. Maybe that comes later. But right now, they're a pair of ghosts—and how do you come to terms with ghosts?"

"You're telling me I ought to go with her to meet him?"

Axel hopped onto a stool and leaned toward her across the snack bar. Leenie finally gave up and looked straight into his eyes. His gray irises were flecked with black and his bronze lashes were short and curly. He smiled. He folded his hands over both of hers and stroked each wristbone with his thumbs.

"You have to make that decision yourself, Leenie. I can't tell you what to do. But I don't like to think of you crawling off into that swamp to hide for all eternity with a bunch of dinosaur bones."

13

"Are you sure he knows we're coming?" Leenie worried out loud.

Hazel had loaned Mary Alice her newly acquired, middle-aged blue station wagon for the trip to Lake City. It was freshly waxed, the inside had been vacuumed, and there were new, bright plaid covers on the front seat. Jemma had sewed Hazel a pair of patchwork bluegills with buttons for eyes that swam cheerfully to and fro on pieces of yarn strung over the rearview mirror.

Leenie felt Mary Alice shoot a fidgety glance her way, then glance back at the highway again. "I called him two days ago, after you agreed to meet him." Mary Alice bit her lip. "I think he's as nervous about this whole thing as you and I are."

You, me, him, Leenie thought. Two more hours and it'll just be us. A couple weeks ago, she'd been living with a widowed grandfather, hadn't had any parents, spent years looking bored when everyone else made Mother's Day or Father's Day cards in grade school. It'd all happened so fast: phone calls to Lake City, agreements reached, dates arranged.

The afternoon sun blazed through the pines at the roadside and slatted the highway with bars of bright and dark. Mary Alice cleared her throat. "I know you think I never loved you, Leenie," she began, "but I meant it when I told your grandfather that I've thought about you almost every day since I left Wayburn sixteen years ago." She hesitated and chewed her lip again. "And in his way, I know your father has, too."

Leenie fingered the plastic trim on the armrest of Hazel's car. "Is my father the one who said blue was the color of faded dreams?" she wondered.

Mary Alice sighed. "No, someone in Boston told me that once. I hope you can meet him sometime."

Him. "You thinking about getting married?"

"I haven't decided yet, Leenie. First, I knew I had to come back to Wayburn and, well, get straight with my past. Yours, too."

Leenie was almost glad the subject of marriage had come up. It gave her a chance to ask about something that'd always bothered her. "Did you guys—you and my father—ever want to get married? To each other, I mean, after you found out you were going to have a baby?"

Mary Alice stroked the steering wheel that Hazel had decorated with an imitation eelskin cover. "We talked about that a little bit, Leenie." A little bit? Not a lot? "But it was too soon for him. For me, too, to tell the truth. Remember, I was only seventeen; he'd just had his eighteenth birthday. Maybe some kids are old enough to be good parents at that age, but that's all we were—just two kids ourselves, who'd accidentally created a child of our own."

Leenie sneaked a glance at Mary Alice; in profile, her nose was short and snubbed, her chin was small and sharp. She tried to imagine what Mary Alice had been like at seventeen. Mostly, she'd been pregnant. Trapped. It must've seemed like a nightmare. But if Allen Lavarty's lips had tasted like sunshine and salt and the moon had been a broken white plate in the sky, maybe it'd been real easy to end up that way.

"We felt terribly guilty about what we'd done," Mary Alice confessed, "especially since we weren't one of those couples who went steady"—she turned and smiled—"that's what it was called back in my day when two kids got real tight. We went around in the same gang, of course, had known each other like forever, and then—well, it just kind of happened." Leenie felt Mary Alice's glance shoot her way again. "Can you understand that?" Mary Alice asked plaintively.

Leenie kept her own gaze on the road. "Kind of," she answered. She closed her eyes to the bars of light and dark on the highway. She felt Axel Erickson's arms against her ribs, the warm, welcome hunger of his lips on her own. But something that felt so good, so right, could end up as a bitter, surprised look in the eye of someone like Gramma, Leenie mused. We never planned on you, that look said; you just came down the road one day and there was nothing we could do but let you in.

"So, anyway, Allen and I made a deal," Mary Alice went on. A deal? Leenie opened her eyes and stared out the car window. First she was a happening, now they were making deals about her, and she hadn't even been born yet?

"As soon as Allen graduated from high school," Mary Alice explained, "he went straight into the Navy. He sent half of his paycheck to me every month in a letter with no return address so no one would know who he was. That's where I got the money for the hospital when you were born. Later, he sent me money so I could start secretarial school up in Boston. He's the one who made it easy for me never to have to show my face in Wayburn again."

Leenie smoothed her jean skirt over her knees. She hadn't worn it all summer; going to see your father for the first time, though, you couldn't wear cut-offs and a T-top. He might not understand about swamp rats. "Did you ever want to keep me?" Leenie asked softly. Or had the bottom line been, after all, that she really was like Harold, just too much trouble to think about having around?

It took Mary Alice a long time to answer. When she did, her voice was small and chokey. "Yes, I did," she whispered finally. "You were such a pretty baby . . . your skin was dark and rosy, your hair was like a little black satin cap . . . but I knew—" She had to pause and collect herself. "So I asked my daddy to take you and raise you up," she went on. "My mother never forgave me, as you already know—maybe it was because she had dreams for me that I never knew about—anyway, I was sure she'd help my father give you a good raising even if she couldn't love you like he did. For sixteen years, Leenie, I've tried to tell myself I did the right thing."

Mary Alice leaned across the plaid expanse of the car seat. When Leenie turned to look into her eyes, it was to see they were filled with tears that Mary Alice was still too proud to shed. "Maybe you did," Leenie heard herself admit. She couldn't add, not yet, maybe not ever, *It's okay; I forgive you.*

It was four o'clock when they arrived in Lake City, a hundred miles from Wayburn. The main street was quiet; it was Friday and some of the stores had closed early for the weekend. "I've arranged to meet your father at his office," Mary Alice murmured, and eased the nose of Hazel's station wagon against a curb.

In the dim, early-morning gloom of the kitchen a week ago, Father Unknown had been given a name; now he had an office. He was slowly developing a whole history. Still, there was so much left to know.

"Is he married now?" Leenie asked. What if he wasn't? There might be a chance, in spite of their bad beginning, that he and Mary Alice could—

But Mary Alice nodded. "Yes, to someone he met while he was in the Navy. It's sort of goofy, but her name is Mary, too!"

"They got any kids?" Those kids will be my half-brothers or half-sisters, Leenie realized with a pang of envy. They'll have everything I never did, like for starters two parents and a last name that won't brand them as being illegitimate. She hoped, with a bitterness that astonished her, that none of them were girls.

"I think he's got three," Mary Alice replied as she turned off the ignition. "Two boys and a girl, as I recall. He sent me their pictures once. The girl looked a lot like you must've at the same age."

"How old is she?" Leenie asked, but dreaded the answer. What if she's fourteen, she worried, really a lot cuter than I'll ever be, already knows how to wear makeup, has so many boyfriends she can't count 'em?

"She's six, I think; Allen said she was in first grade this year." Whew; what a relief! Well, maybe I can learn to like somebody that young, Leenie hoped. Girls that age usually liked dolls; maybe I could give her those that're still on my closet shelf. Sometime, maybe she could visit me; I could show her Sugar Island, teach her how to fish. Her brothers, too.

The building beyond the windshield of Hazel's station wagon was red brick and there was an oak bench and a pot of geraniums beside the entrance. On the smoked glass door several names had been painted in gold; one man was a dentist, another was a lawyer, the last one, in Suite 301, was Allen M. Lavarty, Certified Public Accountant.

If Mary Alice had married him, Leenie realized, I'd be Leenie Lavarty right this very instant. I'd probably be a cheerleader at the Lake City High School and wouldn't know anything at all about a place called Sawmill Swamp or how to pole a punt or catch bluegills. It was eerie to know how close she'd come to being someone entirely different than the person she'd turned out to be. If she'd grown up in Lake City, there'd never have been a Sooz, a Chuckie Bedell, or an Axel Erickson in her life.

The foyer inside the building was silent save for the distant hum of the air conditioning system. Leenie followed Mary Alice up a flight of open stairs and down a hallway. Mary Alice rapped lightly at a door with frosted glass panes, opened it, and motioned Leenie to follow her inside.

"Hello, Allen," she heard Mary Alice say. "I want you to meet our daughter, Arlene." There was a forced, shivery politeness in Mary Alice's voice. "But if you're smart," she warned him in a brittle, over-eager way, "you'll be sure to call her Leenie!"

Leenie tried to arrange her own mouth in a smile. She felt it crack at the corners. Until this particular, frozen moment in time, Father Unknown had floated around in space without a name, a face, a personality. I could pass him anywhere, she used to think, in Decatur or Wayburn or Columbus, and never even know who he was.

Now she stared at the man who stood behind the desk across the room. His tie was loosened and he'd rolled his shirt sleeves up to his elbows. She would've recognized him anywhere.

His face was almost exactly like the one that looked back at her from the mirror every morning when she brushed her teeth. His hair was as unruly as her own and dark as a gypsy's; his hands were bony, like the ones that hung at the ends of her own wrists; his eyes were just about the color of cold coffee.

There was an ice cream stand at the edge of the park across the street from the offices in the Professional Building. There, Allen Lavarty bought three cones. Leenie knew for sure she'd never been to Lake City in her whole life, but its park looked vaguely familiar. She licked her cone and studied the wrought-iron benches along the park paths. Squirrels loudly accused each passerby. An old gentleman sat in the sun, hands folded, growing older. Ah. It was the park from Axel Erickson's photographs.

"Thanks for the cone, uh, ummm—" Leenie began, but couldn't decide how to finish. Should she called him Daddy? Too corny. Mr. Lavarty? Awfully formal. Father, maybe?

"Just call me Allen," Allen Lavarty suggested, and passed a cone to Mary Alice. They walked slowly down the path that circled the park and Leenie searched her mind for a topic that would be reasonably safe to talk about.

"What's your little girl's name?" she asked politely. It was all so weird. He's *my* father, too, Leenie thought, not only the dad of some little girl I don't even know yet. And how would she explain this whole afternoon to Sooz—or should she even try?

"Her name's Mollie," Allen answered. Mollie; it was a real sweet name, a name hard to be jealous of. Leenie and Mollie—actually, they sounded like the names of two girls who were sisters, who sometime might even be friends.

"Someday I hope you can meet my whole family," Allen went on, "but I guess you realize there're things that'll have to be ironed out first.

What I mean is, you know all about them, but they still don't know anything about you."

Leenie bit into her cone; the crunch sounded as loud as a cannon in her ears. How would he explain her? Would he sit his wife down some night after supper, after the kids had gone to bed, and say, "I have something important to tell you, Mary. Our daughter Mollie isn't the only daughter I have." No matter what he said, the news would cause shock waves Leenie didn't want to think about.

Under his ruddy tan, Allen had turned pink. "It's going to be real embarrassing at first," he admitted. There were threads of gray at his temples, Leenie noticed, and a vein throbbed steadily behind his ear. He studied his ice cream cone with more attention than it deserved.

"And even after my family knows about you, Leenie, it still might be hard for all of us. You, me, them. It might be a big mistake to believe this'll necessarily be one of those happily-ever-after kind of stories."

"But you didn't have to let me come here today," Leenie reminded him. "So how come you did?"

Allen considered a distant row of sycamores on the edge of the park as if they might offer up an answer. "I guess it was because of Mollie," he said finally. When he turned to look at her, Leenie saw an expression both hopeful and apologetic in his coffee-colored glance.

"You see, she's my youngest child—the boys are ten and twelve—but every time I looked at Mollie, I had to remember she wasn't the only daughter I had. Mollie's got everything a little girl could want—a mom and dad, two brothers who love her—but I knew you didn't even know who I was. A year ago, when Mary Alice wrote to me about you, I realized I owed you at least that much.''

Leenie sat down on the last bench at the edge of the park. A moment later, Mary Alice sat down beside her. Finally, Allen sat down, too. Two squirrels quarreled near the base of an oak tree nearby; across the park, Leenie could see Axel's old gentleman dozing in the afternoon sun.

Here I am, she marveled, in Lake City, with my mother sitting on one side of me and my father on the other. Lake City is only a hundred miles from Wayburn, but I might as well be on the moon. Having gone to the moon, nothing will ever be the same again. Maybe the story didn't really have to have a storybook ending, either.

Leenie cleared her throat. ''Listen, you guys, it's going to be okay,'' she told Mary Alice and Allen. She was tempted to reach for their hands, so the three of them could sit there, connected. She kept her fingers laced together in her lap. ''What I mean is, life isn't pasteurized and homogenized,'' she explained. ''Sometimes it doesn't have vitamin D added and won't meet all daily minimum requirements. So what? We'll get along with what we've got. I just have this feeling we can.'' Allen smiled a little; Mary Alice finished her cone.

14

As soon as Mary Alice pulled the station wagon into the driveway at the Dew Drop Inn, Leenie jumped out and hurried down the twilit path to cabin twelve. Axel must've already gone to bed because the cabin was dark. But he won't mind getting waked up to hear about this, Leenie decided; he'd want to hear how her life was getting glued together, that Allen had eyes the color of cold coffee and wanted her to meet his other family someday.

Leenie rapped on the door. No answer came from inside. She rapped a little louder. Starlight glimmered on the doorknob, windowsills, made the cinder path glitter dully. She tried the door. It opened; she reached in to flick on the kitchen light

There was no clothesline rope on the door handles of the cupboards. The stacks of photographs were gone from the snack bar. Leenie glanced through the archway into the half-darkened living room. There was no picture of Jane on the coffee table. Leenie tiptoed, unwilling to believe Axel was gone, too, to the bedroom and bath. Ruth or Eloise had freshly made up the bed; the bath was empty of developing trays and photo enlarger.

Leenie slumped onto a stool beside the snack bar. Why hadn't he waited? They still had so much to say to one another. Or was she the only one left with anything to say?

Cabin twelve didn't seem nearly as dear and cozy as it used to. Leenie cupped her chin in her palm. Maybe it would help if she heated up some water and made a pot of tea. She filled the kettle, turned the front burner to high, opened the cupboard to reach for her secret stash of tea bags that most tourist occupants never found.

Propped against a cup was a yellow envelope with her name on it. Had she told Axel about coming here to drink tea sometimes? Maybe she had, along with all the other stuff she'd told him about herself out there in the swamp.

Leenie fished the note out of the envelope. His handwriting was brisk, and she could hear his easy-to-listen-to voice as she read. "*Dear Leenie,*" he began, "*Jane called to tell me she's finished her book and that's the reason I'm taking off in such a hurry. I left all your photos with Hazel. When I come back from England, I'll get to work on my (our?) book about swamps and you'll be the first to get a copy when it's printed. Thanks for everything, Leenie. You're a very special person to me. My address is at the bottom of this letter; please write and let me know how your day in Lake City went. Love, Axel.*"

Leenie traced his signature with her finger. *Love, Axel.* He didn't mean love, she knew, not like in moon-June-my-heart's-on-fire-with-desire love. Leenie poured hot water over her tea bag and let it steep. But maybe he did love me in a way, she decided. Maybe I loved him the same way, only out there on the island I didn't exactly know the difference between love and wanting to hang on to someone.

Lucy pressed her nose against the screen and begged to be let in. Leenie slipped her clogs off and opened the door with her bare toe. "Glad to see me, mutt?" Leenie asked. Lucy McGee wagged an admission that she was. Leenie sipped her tea. In ten days, school would start; in two months, the season would be over. She finished her tea slowly, washed the cup, put it away. She was pretty sure she had enough money saved from lifeguarding all summer to buy a camera. Maybe Mary Alice would like to go to Wayburn tomorrow to help pick one out.

Two days later, it was Mary Alice's turn to leave. She dressed up in her lavender suit and her pretty, strappy sandals and looked almost like the same person who'd arrived three weeks earlier. She couldn't quite resign herself, though, to the fact that the O'Briens might never be a regular family.

"Maybe we don't have to be," Leenie tried to explain. "Maybe it's okay if we're just the way we are. Kind of irregular."

"But I really want to make things up to you," Mary Alice insisted, "and besides, Boston is a wonderful place to live! There are so many things to do—and Boston even has lots of water!" she added, as if the promise of water might lure Leenie away.

"Maybe I can come up later for a visit," Leenie murmured, careful not to attach a time and a date to the offer. She recalled the fib she'd told Axel about being an orphan and having to leave the Dew Drop forever, also Sugar Island, Lucy, Granda, and Hazel, which she knew perfectly well she'd never do. She couldn't actually imagine leaving any of them, not even to go to Boston to live with her own mother.

There. She'd thought the thought: my . . . own . . . mother. Eventually she'd be able to say it, even know what it really meant.

"Anyway, I'm glad you came back to Wayburn," Leenie sighed as they waited beside the road. "I was shook up at first," she admitted, "because I didn't know what to expect. But now we can start to write back and forth, just like maybe sometimes I can write to Allen."

Mary Alice swung her purse idly back and forth, like a schoolgirl. Now that the moment to leave had arrived, she seemed to be happy to be on her way. "Life's funny, isn't it?" she mused.

"A real riot," Leenie agreed. She could hear the Wayburn bus turn at the junction of Highway 82 and County Road 12. She'd felt shy about taking Mary Alice's hand when they were in Lake City, but now she reached out. Mary Alice's fingers were slim and cool against her own, and when her mother turned, her eyes were shiny with proud O'Brien tears that might never be shed. After she got on the bus, however, Mary Alice pressed her hand against the green-tinted window and mouthed the words *I love you.*

Leenie hesitated. *I think I love you, too,* she mouthed back. It was too early to promise anything for sure. It was pretty hard to make love happen till it was ready. Like Allen Lavarty said, it might be a mistake to believe their story was one of those happily-ever-after kind.

Hazel fixed spare ribs with molasses-and-orange sauce for supper. "Too bad Mary Alice couldn't have stayed for one more meal with us," she lamented. "My, that girl sure used to love old Hazel's ribs!"

"Speaking of old Hazel's ribs," Leenie observed slyly, poking an index finger against Hazel's own, "seems to me these right here are getting kind of lean. You taking a few feathers out of your pillow, Hazel?"

Hazel deposited herself in a chair and began to shell some peas. "I want to look spiffy in my new dress," she huffed, lowering her butterscotch gaze. "Not that it's any business of yours."

"Dress!" Leenie exclaimed, shocked. "Never in my entire life have I seen you in a dress, Hazel Grobey!"

"Well, there's no law in this county that says I can't wear one. Besides, that's what ladies usually wear to dances."

"You're going to a dance? Who with?"

"None of your beeswax."

"C'mon, Hazel—the truth." Leenie slumped into a chair herself and folded her arms on the table top. She was pretty sure she knew what had happened. Hazel had met someone who liked to go fishing as well as she did; she probably wanted to settle down again, might quit working at the Dew Drop, would become a stranger you only waved at when you met her in Wayburn. "C'mon," Leenie groaned, missing Hazel already, "the truth, please."

"All right, already." Peas popped crisply out of their shells into the bowl in Hazel's wide lap. "Your granddaddy and I have signed up for some square dancing lessons. There's a bunch of folks in town about our age—they call themselves the Pie R Squares—and we thought it'd be a tickle to get acquainted with 'em."

Leenie sat up eagerly. "You and Granda got something going? Any chance you might decide to get married someday?"

"Leenie, Leenie. Quit, girl. We are only going square dancing. We're not going to get a license to do anything else."

Leenie slumped again. "I just always thought it'd be so nice if you guys would—" she began lamely.

Hazel reached across the table and caught both of Leenie's hands in one of her own large brown ones. "Endings like that are mainly for books, sweet cakes," she murmured gently. "In real life, most of us have to settle for something that isn't quite as tidy."

"But wouldn't it be neat if you never had to go home anymore as soon as you got through with supper dishes?" Leenie pleaded. "And I bet Granda would let you raise as many tomatoes as you wanted, even eggplant, though he doesn't like it much. We three could be so—you know, happy."

Hazel shrugged a still-hefty shoulder. "We *are* happy, sweet cakes. You could be, too, if you'd just quit trying to live other peoples' lives for them."

The yellow bowl in Hazel's lap was half-full of green peas. Leenie reached over and helped herself to a few. Maybe Hazel was right. I even tried to live Sooz's and Chuckie's lives for them, Leenie reflected, not to mention Mary Alice's and Allen Lavarty's. I'll quit, she decided. Tonight. Tonight there'll be spare ribs for supper, plus fresh peas, and she was sure she'd seen a peach pie in the fridge. She'd let that be enough for now.

Leenie could see the tin roof of the cabin wink in the September sun like a silver eye. When she eased the boat ashore, she could see that the magnolia tree beside the porch had lost all its blooms and the reeds at the island's edge were turning brown. The swamp would soon get ready for a winter's sleep; the turtles and snakes would begin to hibernate in the muck; some of the birds would migrate to Mexico, some even as far away as the mountains of Peru.

She walked slowly up the path toward the cabin. She hadn't been back on the island since she left it with Axel. She mounted the bottom step of the porch, turned just as she had the night she'd found herself kissing him, holding him like she never wanted to let him go. For a fleeting moment Leenie felt his lips on hers, felt his kisses on her wrists, felt him hold her away.

You're older than you think you are, he'd reminded her.

It was true. Why hadn't she realized that herself? Even Huckleberry Finn had to grow up sometime. She couldn't be a tomboy named Leenie forever and ever. "Arlene O'Brien," Leenie said out loud, trying on her proper name. It didn't sound too bad. "Arlene O'Brien, Deputy Assistant, U.S. Fish and Game Department," Leenie ventured. That was even better. Putting the past behind you probably didn't mean you had to give up everything. The one person she'd never be was Leenie Lavarty, though. She'd never be exactly legal. Somehow, that fact didn't hurt quite so much anymore.

Inside the cabin, Leenie brushed mouse droppings off the peach-crate shelf and rearranged the bent silverware, the tin plates, the plastic water jugs. Maybe next summer Mollie and her brothers could come out here. Kids that age would be crazy about a cabin on an island! They'd get brown as little berries; they'd go fishing every day. She'd teach them everything she knew. First, though, Allen would have to explain *her* to his family. She wondered if he would start by saying. . . . Then she gave herself a mental pinch. There you go again, Leenie warned herself—living other people's lives!

When the cabin was cleaned up, Leenie whistled for Lucy, closed the door, and fastened the hasp in place. After Lucy boarded the *Swamp Rat,* Leenie pushed off from shore and began to pole out of the swamp. I'll have to find a new name for the boat, she decided. She searched her mind for a name that reflected how things were now. How about the *Moll-Lee,* the combined names of two sisters who might someday be friends? "The *Moll-Lee,*" Leenie said out loud. It sounded exactly right.

The doorbell in Granda's office bleated fretfully. Not many tourists showed up this late in the season, but any who did were more than welcome. Leenie bounded to the door and arranged a bright Chamber-of-Commerce smile on her face. But it was Chuckie Bedell on the step with a cardboard box under his arm. His Honda was parked at the side of the road.

"You lost, Chuckie?" Leenie asked, and deftly removed her smile.

"Nope. I gotta deliver this to you." He hefted the box under his arm. "Would've come sooner only we've been busy at the shelter."

"The shelter?"

"The animal shelter. I work there three afternoons a week." Chuckie inclined his blond head toward the Honda. He needed a fresh perm, Leenie noticed. "I gotta pay for the bike somehow," he said, grinning. She'd forgotten what a cute smile he had.

"What's in the box?" Leenie murmured.

"Our last orphan. A guy stopped by two weeks ago and bailed him out. Told me to bring him out here. Said you'd understand."

Leenie peered through a round air hole that had been cut in the top of the box. A pair of mild pink eyes peered back at her out of a furry white face.

"Harold? Is that Harold in there?" Leenie squealed. "What'd he say?"

"Actually, I don't believe I've ever heard Harold talk at all," Chuckie answered.

"Not Harold, dopus—I mean the guy who bailed him out." Only one person in the world could've sprung Harold and sent him to the Dew Drop.

Chuckie squinted skyward. "Let me think. I guess he said something about not hiding out with dinosaur bones. He said you'd know right away what he meant." Chuckie passed Harold to her, then shifted his weight from one foot to the other.

"So, anyway, how've you been?" he wanted to know. "Nobody's seen you practically all summer."

Leenie held Harold's box against her middle. "I've been real busy," she sighed, "lifeguarding, fishing, the usual." It would get entirely too complicated to explain about Axel and the twelfth of never.

"You want to take a spin on the Honda?" Chuckie asked. "She's a Goldwing GL 1200, a real sweet machine."

Leenie hesitated. "I probably better not," she murmured. "Sooz might get ticked, since you two are so—"

"Past tense, Leen. We're Splitsville. She took up with Jason Bates."

"But I thought Jason and Melissa were still—"

"How long you been gone, Leen? They're done with each other. Now you want to run into Wayburn or not? We could see what's up, who's at Walser's, like that."

"I'll have to get Harold settled down first."

"Right. Let me give you a hand."

Leenie let Chuckie carry Harold toward the garage. Granda would have to build a pen; they'd buy some rabbit pellets; Lucy would have to get used to having Harold for a buddy. If the two of them had a hard time getting along, Leenie decided, she'd just sit them down and explain life to them. Listen, you guys, she'd say, remember, the rainbow comes and goes.

PATRICIA CALVERT, who lives in Chatfield, Minnesota, is a senior editorial assistant in the Section of Publications of the Mayo Clinic. She holds a degree in history, is working on a master's degree in children's literature, and is the author of several young adult novels.